# DAYKEEPER

ISBN-13: 978-0578519562

45 Alternate Press, LLC
Hampton, VA

# DAYKEEPER

RAN WALKER

ALTERNATE 45 PRESS

*Running from the daylight*
*To where she keeps me...*

— The Foreign Exchange

# CHAPTER ONE

NOTHING SMELLS WORSE THAN THE SCENT OF impending death. It's like the sour before the rot. The perfume doesn't cover it, but I smile as if it does.

As my wife sleeps, I stare at her, taking in her appearance, remembering when her body was full and beautiful, her hair long and wavy, her eyes full of wonder. Now cancer has stripped her of her glow, leaving her body gaunt, her eyes distant, and what is left of her hair wrapped beneath a faded scarf. And I have never loved her more than I do right now.

I trace my index finger around her thin hands and smile at their warmth.

Her doctor gave her a month to live. We are now in month three.

That's my Charlotte, my wife of fifteen years, my better half. I was finishing my master's degree and preparing for my PhD in African-American studies when I wandered into a jazz club on a Friday night and fell in love with the woman singing lead. Her voice enveloped me like the sensual hug of a woman capable of only the most powerful love, and my eyes were immediately drawn to her. She moved like no one I had ever seen, and she had me with every word, every nod of her head, every wave of her hand. She made me her fan within minutes—and I didn't even know her name. Thankfully, she accepted my offer to buy her a drink, or I probably wouldn't be sitting next to her now, watching her sleep, not wanting her to suffer, but not wanting her to leave me.

"Hey, let's take a walk," my brother, Marcus, offers. He places his hand on my shoulder, as if to suggest that it's OK for me to leave my wife's side for a moment.

I follow him through the house, passing my wife's parents and her two sisters. They don't care much for me, and my apathy towards their dislike hasn't made matters any better. But today we are united through Charlotte, and as long as we are united through our fear of losing her, we have an unspoken truce.

Marcus walks out into the driveway and immediately pulls a cigarette from the box in his shirt pocket. He's been itching for a smoke, I can tell. He puffs a few times before he speaks.

"It's good to stretch your legs, you know?"

I nod. The sky is clear and beautiful, but the air feels thin, empty.

He offers me a cigarette. I stare longingly at the pack. I haven't smoked since I first started dating Charlotte, nearly seventeen years ago. Charlotte viewed smoking as a professional hazard because of her voice. Staring at the pack, I contemplate taking one—just to take some of the edge off of the day, but I shake my head and look away.

Marcus doesn't say anything. We just stand in the driveway staring off into the distance. There's not much to say. The fact that he has flown across the country to support his little brother is enough.

———

WITH THE SUN setting behind us, Marcus and I walk back into the house to find the living room and den empty. My heart drops, and I immediately fear the worse. Pushing past Marcus to reach the master bedroom, I see Charlotte's parents and sisters standing beside the bed. I stop breathing and slowly look toward my Charlotte. Her scarf has been replaced with one of her performance wigs and her face has been made up. She looks almost like she did the first moment I saw her. She smiles at me, and I feel my heart melt.

Taking a seat on the bed next to her, I lean over and kiss her repeatedly. "I love you so much," I say, blinking away the tears filling my eyes.

"I love you too, Ed." Her voice is soft, frail.

"We can fight this, baby," I say, kissing each of her hands in turn. "We're gonna make it."

She smiles at me, tears in her eyes. She has only seen me cry once, when our son, Edward, Jr., was stillborn.

A fear descends over me. I am not ready to lose my best friend.

"Eddie," she whispers.

"Yes, baby," I answer, leaning in closely. She has never called me Eddie before, and it sounds strange coming from her lips.

"Eddie." Her voice is now faint.

"Yes, baby."

"Eddie," she says softly, looking past me. "Mommy's coming."

# CHAPTER TWO

---

I DO NOT HEAR THE PASTOR DELIVERING THE eulogy. I do not even notice the flowers laid atop the closed casket. The only thing I notice, between my trembling hands, is a beautiful photograph of my wife on delicate linen stock. Beneath her face are the dates 1975-2013. Thirty-eight years. I had been married to her fifteen of those years.

We lived within the dash between those dates, our marriage occupying the pages of her short life. I want so badly to hold her, if only to keep my insides from caving in on themselves. Instead, I must watch as the pallbearers carry her casket from the church to the hearse. I trail behind her, my brother helping to keep me on my feet, his strong arms lifting me.

"Ashes to ashes, dust to dust," the pastor whispers, sprinkling a handful of Georgia clay upon her casket.

I stay to watch as the casket is lowered into the ground. It is only when my brother awakens me late in the evening that I realize I have fallen asleep next to the tombstone with an empty bottle of Johnnie Walker Black Label lying next to me.

---

DAY AND NIGHT run into endless, painful hours. The curtains in the den seal out the light, while the air conditioner blasts air so cold that I curl myself beneath a comforter draped across the couch. I wake occasionally to eat a microwave dinner or can of soup or to use the bathroom.

Sometimes in the darkness I pray that she will appear to me so that I can tell her how much I miss her. I am, however, only met with the stillness of this old house, the constant reminder that I am alone, no matter what I would want to believe to the contrary.

---

I TOOK a leave of absence from Ellison-Wright College during the spring semester of 2013, with plans to return in the fall, but losing my wife has proved to be harder than anything I have ever had to do. The future is unclear now, and I spend my days contemplating what it means to be alone after fifteen years of being married to such an amazing woman.

Sometimes the guilt creeps over me as I remember Charlotte's dreams and how I had hindered her from achieving them. She only wanted to sing. She bounced around the South with me as I went from teaching position to teaching position, always in search of something better. When we had finally made it here to Atlanta, she had had a year of open mics before the doctor diagnosed the lump in her breast as malignant. After that, she stopped performing and started giving voice lessons out of our home in Fairburn. Sometimes at night, when she didn't know I was watching, she would curl up on the couch beneath an afghan she had made while we were dating and listen to Minnie Riperton's "Inside My Love." That was her favorite song, and the irony of my wife suffering from the same illness as Minnie was difficult to ignore. I would watch her lips tremble as she sang along quietly. As Minnie's high-pitched voice blended into the lush keyboards of the breakdown, I would ease up next to Charlotte and wrap my arms around her. She would quickly wipe her eyes and turn to face me, singing with a voice that was beautifully rich and personal. It was the performance that she reserved for me, the part that she wanted me to remember most.

Now, sitting here, cloaked in darkness, her melodic voice whispering inside my head, I know that she had ultimately sacrificed her dream for me. That awareness leaves an inconsolable pain.

I lift the old afghan to my face, inhaling as much of her as I can, while trying to outrun the guilt I feel burrowing itself into my gut. I wish I could evaporate into this sadness and disappear.

---

THE PHONE RINGS, waking me. I feel for it in the blackness of the room. My fingers touch it, and I contemplate whether or not to answer.

Marcus's name flashes across the screen, so I answer.

"Ed?"

"Yeah," I manage, fumbling to place the phone next to my face.

"Ed, you there?"

"Yeah."

"Did you get my calls, man?"

"Huh?"

"I've been leaving messages for you the past few days. Did you get any of them?"

"Uh," I say, trying to remember if I had heard the phone ring. "Nah, I don't think so."

"Yeah, man. I've been calling you. I figured you just needed some time to yourself, you know?"

"Um-hmm," I say sitting up on the couch, more alert now.

"How are you doing?"

I stare around the room and realize that I can't really make out anything. "I'm alive, I guess."

"You guess? Ed, you've gotta open up your curtains."

"What are you talking about?"

"You've gotta let some light in."

"What do you mean?"

Suddenly I hear the doorbell ringing. I stand up, dressed only in my boxers and a t-shirt. I walk cautiously toward the door.

"Is that you?" I ask.

"Yeah. Open the door."

I open it slowly, squinting at the sunlight coming through the crack. I can barely make out the silhouette of my brother in the doorway.

"You came back all this way?" I ask.

"I've been worried about you, and when you didn't answer, I figured you might need a little help." He peers through the door into the madness that has become my home. "And by the look of it, I'm not a second too soon."

# CHAPTER THREE

The smell of coffee fills my three-bedroom house. I know it must be a Kenyan blend or something on the upper end, because Marcus doesn't do Maxwell House. To me, they all smell the same. But then, I don't drink coffee.

That doesn't stop him from placing a mug in front of me.

"I put some cream and sugar in there, since I know how you are about coffee," he says, sitting down across from me.

I nod and take a sip, allowing the hot liquid to sting my tongue. I want to feel alive, so I hold it in my mouth before swallowing.

"How long has it been since you left the house?" he asks.

"Don't know. Since I got back from the funeral."

"Come on, Ed. We've gotta get you some air. You can suffocate in here like this."

"I've got air conditioning."

"Yeah, but that's not what I'm talking about—and you know it."

I take another sip and stare at the mug to avoid making eye contact.

"You've been in this house for ten days straight?" he

asks in disbelief, as if the math has finally dawned on him. "Get a shower. We're going out. Now!"

I don't feel like moving, but I know he's right. "Where are we going?"

"Don't worry about that. We're gonna just get some fresh air, little brother. Trust me. It'll be cool."

I stand slowly, feeling unsteady, my legs still a little weak from lying down for so long. "OK."

I walk back to the bathroom I have not showered in since the morning of the funeral. Turning the knobs and adjusting the showerhead, I undress and step into the hot water. It blasts me between my shoulder blades, welcoming me back into the present.

The feeling is surreal, this loneliness. I allow the water to run between my fingers, across my face, and through my unkempt hair. Charlotte would not like me now: not taking care of myself. She would tell me that *her* man had to measure up to Denzel, or preferably exceed him, a comment that would always make me smile.

"Damn, baby, I miss you so much," I mutter, my eyes closed as the water runs down my face.

I stand beneath the water until it begins to run cold and my fingertips draw up like raisins. I know I will step out of the shower and grab my towel and that everything will be different, but for the moment I stand still, remembering what it was.

———

THE FIRST STOP on my brother's planned excursion is a trip to the barbershop down the street from my house, where, upon entry, he immediately yells out to no one in particular, "Emergency! We need someone right now to shave the mane off Beast Man here!" Everyone laughs, and the old man in the corner looks at me curiously, nodding his agreement.

A kid probably half my age beckons me to his chair, and my brother, again speaking for me, gives a simple instruction: "Cut all that shit off! All of it!"

The kid leans down and looks at me. "Sir, you want me to take it all off?"

I try to muster a smile and be a good sport. I couldn't care less either way. I nod my head. "Sure."

The clippers are on my head before I can close my mouth.

---

THE LAST TIME I wore a bald head was when I was pledging my college fraternity. I didn't particularly like it at the time, although I was told that I had a head for it—unlike my Tail, who had these curious brain-like grooves all across his scalp. Charlotte had never seen my hair any shorter than a low Caesar cut. She loved to run her fingers through my waves.

Driving toward Buckhead, Marcus comments on my appearance.

"You're looking good, Ed."

"Yeah?"

"I'm telling you. That haircut has you looking ten years younger."

"Well, I feel ten years older."

He looks away, pretending to concentrate on his driving.

I'm glad that Marcus is here, but he doesn't understand what it means to lose your better half. He has never been married and professes to enjoy the single life so much that he could never think of settling down. I appreciate what he's trying to do, but I'd rather be at home under the covers, alone with my thoughts.

"We're going out to eat tonight. OK?" he says.

I nod.

"I have to get back tomorrow morning for a meeting, and I promised to take out this hot little flight attendant who hooked me up with the plane tickets to get back here."

I smile. That sounds just like my brother: dating a woman to use her flight passes. But he's here for me, and for the first time I wonder what I will do when he leaves again.

---

DINNER IS AT JEAN-LOUIS, a Cajun spot off of Old National Highway. Marcus likes to eat here whenever he's in town. Apparently they don't have restaurants like this in his area of San Jose. We get a seat outside on the patio beneath a large forest green umbrella. The view is nice and the warmth of the May air is pleasant, but I'm not very hungry.

Marcus ends up ordering for both of us, and while I don't know if my stomach is ready for jambalaya, the spiciness might be the very thing I need to snap out of this daze.

"I can't even begin to imagine what you must feel right now," he starts.

I don't want him to finish, but I am too tired to interject.

He continues, "I loved my sister-in-law, and you know this. And you and I both know she wouldn't want to see you moping around sad all the time."

"She just died!" I almost yell out, before catching myself and softening the words.

"I know, Ed. I know. But she would want to know that you could still smile, that you could still enjoy life."

It had been a little over two weeks since Marcus and I had stood outside my house, while my wife's sisters had prepared her to see me that last time. It feels like yesterday and a lifetime ago at the same time. I am suddenly confused. I don't know how I should feel. I only know that I hurt.

The meal is delicious, and I find myself relaxing a little, enjoying the sound of my brother's voice, as he talks about the different projects his tech consulting company is working on. As I take a sip of the my iced sweet tea, I see his eyes move beyond me.

"Play along," he whispers.

"What?"

Before I can turn my head, several smiling employees surround me. The young lady in the middle of the group is holding a slice of chocolate cake with a candle on top. They sing their version of the birthday song, as she places the cake directly in front of me.

"Make a wish," she says, smiling.

In that brief moment, I see something in her eyes, and she reminds me so much of Charlotte. I gasp, before blowing out the candle.

"Happy birthday, little brother!" Marcus says, his wide grin taking up most of his face.

I laugh. I turned forty back in January, but I relish the cake like today is actually my birthday. May, January, close enough.

As my brother takes care of the check, the young lady who brought me the cake returns to the table.

"I hope you have a wonderful birthday," she says. Her smile is warm and sweet, and while she doesn't actually look like Charlotte, she exudes the kind of warmth that Charlotte did.

"Thank you," I respond, looking at her nametag. "Thank you, Tanya."

As I follow my brother out of the restaurant, he leans over and whispers to me, "You're gonna be all right, little brother. Trust me."

# CHAPTER FOUR

No. 1

*Parted blinds shift shadows across dusty floors*
*as this house wakes to another morning*
*of my steps echoing through an empty*
*foyer, missing the rhythm of her feet,*
*this heart beating out of sync, longing*
*for a melody that once sang as*
*sweetly as the croon of Nina's voice.*

No. 2

*Rose petals wither atop cold, mussed sheets,*
*while I make my bed on stiff*
*sofas, stacks of books keeping me company,*
*mute words saying nothing to quell this*
*empty heart that died against your pillow.*
*Still I ponder what it means to be*
*alone, a widower, a shell, a half.*

## CHAPTER FIVE

TWO MONTHS HAVE PASSED SINCE MY BROTHER returned to California, and I have begun to discover a few things about myself. I have discovered that it's OK to walk outside and enjoy the feel of the sun dancing upon my face and that I can still laugh and smile and dance, when the mood hits. But I have also discovered that I will always miss my wife, no matter how normal things may appear on the surface.

I am also writing again. Nothing major. Just the occasional poem or short story. I am determined to return to work this fall, simply because I am starting to yearn for the feeling of being around people and having a purpose. I have already started preparing the syllabi for the two courses I will be teaching. The faculty convenes in three weeks, and I plan to walk into that first meeting with my head lifted high, no matter how I might actually feel.

Marvin Gaye's "I Want You" plays softly in the background, as I thumb through my notebook. My fingers stop on two Kwansabas I wrote over the past few days. I have fallen in love with this poetic form and its seven lines/ seven words per line/ seven letters (or less) per word structure. I was even fortunate enough to have a few of my poems published by its creator, Dr.

Eugene Redmond, in his literary journal, *Drumvoices Revue*, during the semester before I took my leave. Now it has become one of the main ways I express my feelings about all that is going on in my head.

*No. 6*

> *I often watch my shadow leaning away*
> *from who I was to become—alone.*
> *Cognac and faded photos of our life*
> *swirl behind closed lids, calling me away*
> *to be with you, camped in the nook*
> *of your neck, your perfume alive*
> *in each nostril, as I breathe you.*

*No. 7*

> *I see you in the crimson tulips,*
> *waving in the gusts of spring breezes,*
> *and I long to feel the magic*
> *of your words tickle my thoughts like*
> *a feather softly brushed across the sole*
> *of a baby's tiny foot or the*
> *high pitched laugh of being in love.*

I CAN FEEL Charlotte in the words scribbled across each page. I say them aloud, like an incantation, hoping that there is at least a small piece of magic than can resurrect her energy into this space. Marvin croons in the background, and I reach out, hoping against reality that my hands will not meet the emptiness of the room.

———

NOT WANTING to feel the loneliness of this house, I

have been trying out hobbies that will get me out of the house. The only one that seems to be sticking is going to the gym. We had memberships for the past few years, and at one time we worked out regularly. Pretty soon "regularly" became "occasionally," and before Charlotte became sick, we had all but given up going. It was just a forgotten deduction coming out of our bank account each month. Now it has become the one thing that is helping to keep me sane.

But on some days it feels like I am about to fall off the edge of a cliff. I sometimes walk around the entire day in anticipation, sensing the beat of my own heart, feeling more mortal than any sane person should. The photo album containing our wedding pictures rests on the nightstand by the bed, and I look at them each night before I go to sleep in hopes that I will dream about her. But I never do.

# CHAPTER SIX

I AM SITTING ON ONE OF THE LARGE, CUSHY armchairs suited more for sleeping than reading, incognegro in the back of JoAnne's Books and Java, when I see her. She looks slightly different with her dark, curly hair blown into a frizzy Afro. The last time I saw her, it was pulled back into a bushy ponytail and she was holding a piece of chocolate birthday cake, an unwitting aid to my brother's practical joke. Her name comes to my tongue immediately: Tanya.

Her face is beautiful in a subtle way, her brown complexion a few shades lighter than my own. Her head rests against the palm of her right hand, as she studies a book. She adjusts the thin rectangular glasses perched on the edge of her nose. A small amber amulet hangs around her neck, just above the scoop neck of her crème colored shirt, emphasizing the fullness of her chest and the contrast between her skin tone and the fabric. I don't realize I am staring at her until I suddenly become aware she is looking back at me. I quickly avert my eyes, returning them to my book, the heat of embarrassment circling my face as if I'm standing too close to an oven.

Uncomfortably, I walk over to the café area, just to create some distance between me and the awkwardness

I had just created. I order a strawberry and banana smoothie, taking a seat at one of the small tables nearby. I sip my drink and try to lose myself in the book I have been carrying around the store with no intention of purchasing.

Out the corner of my eye, I see Tanya standing at the counter, placing an order. I don't know what it is about her that reminds me of Charlotte, because they hardly resemble each other. Maybe it's the way she carries herself.

She lifts her coffee cup from the counter and walks toward me.

"Is it OK if I sit here?" she asks.

My teeth quickly let go of my straw, and I can feel some of the pink-colored smoothie smearing across my bottom lip. Embarrassed, I quickly brush it away with a napkin. "Sure."

"How are you doing, Dr. Nelson?"

My eyebrow involuntarily rises. "How did you know my name?"

"I'm a student at Ellison-Wright. Don't worry. I haven't had your class, so I wouldn't expect you to know my name."

"Tanya," I say.

"Impressive." Her smile is broad enough for her dimples to dance beneath the light of the café.

"Well, I'm good with names. I remembered your nametag from Jean-Louis. What's your classification?"

"Rising junior. I'm majoring in mass communications."

"That must be interesting," I respond.

"What do you mean?"

"That's Donaldson's department. I hear he runs a pretty tight ship over there."

She laughs. Even her laughter is refreshing. "No offense, but that guy is crazy."

I have had my own run-ins with Albert Donaldson,

and I avoid him at all costs. But I don't tell her this, because I don't speak ill of other professors to students. Instead, I let her speak, while I listen.

"He's the only professor teaching Senior Thesis this fall, and everyone is flipping out. I hope he's not the only one teaching it next fall. I don't know if I could deal with having him as a professor. You know, they say he only gives out five A's. It's like some funky curve where half the class fails. Crazy, right?"

I smile. "Well, you should have majored in African-American Studies. We could've spared you the heartache."

"Yeah, maybe," she says. She takes a sip of her coffee. "Hey, I'm really sorry to hear about your wife."

I expect the comment to sting, but it doesn't. I feel strangely numb. "Thank you."

As she takes another sip, I wait anxiously to see if my wife's passing will become the focus of our conversation—because if it does, I might not be able to take it. Thankfully, she shifts topics and asks if I am returning in the fall.

"Yes. I'll be teaching two courses?"

"Oh really? Which ones?"

"Survey of Contemporary African-American Literature and Intro to African-American Studies?"

"I wish I had known that you'd be teaching them. I might've taken one as an elective," she says. She smiles, rotating the cup in her hands.

"Don't worry. I'll probably teach the second part of the courses in the spring, and since there are no prerequisites, you could just jump right in, if you wanted to."

She chuckles. "I might have to do that."

I sip from my smoothie, suddenly self-conscious of how ridiculous a man can look with his lips wrapped around a small straw, sucking away. Her presence is comforting, though, and I realize this is the first real conversation I have had with anyone outside of Marcus, since the funeral.

"Where are you from?" I ask.

"Houston. H-Town," she says, before adding, "well, you know, that's what we call it."

"I know H-Town," I respond. "I also know that it gets hot as hell down there."

"Who you tellin'?" she says, laughing. "I used to be light-skinned when I was little."

"You're not that far off of light skinned now."

"Yes, I am. I'm like the color of a young Michael Jackson now."

"Well, it suits you well," I say, not meaning to flirt, but suddenly feeling that I might be.

"Thanks," she responds, pausing to check something on her cell phone. "Give me a second."

The fact that she is still sitting at my table is making the situation all the more surreal. She is not my student, nor do I have any real connection to her, yet she is content to converse with me, a man twice her age, a widower. I am curious how much longer this conversation will last before she leaves to join people her own age.

"Hey, Dr. Nelson," she says, breaking into my thoughts. "I have to run and pick up one of my girls. Her man is trippin'."

"I understand."

She stands to leave and pauses for a moment. "Do you have WEB Instant Messenger?"

It takes me a second to realize what she's talking about. My brother sometimes sends me instant messages, but I rarely use it for anything else. "Yes," I respond.

"What's your handle?"

"Professor Ed, but it's all one word."

She nods, punching the information into her

phone. "Professored," she says, making my handle into an adjective. " I like that. OK. I'll talk to you later."

I nod as she walks away, tossing what's left of her coffee into the garbage can.

I don't understand what just took place, but I sense she might have just done the equivalent of asking for my phone number.

"Oh, lord," I sigh. What have I just gotten myself into?

# CHAPTER SEVEN

*No. 19*
> *I usually dream of you, but tonight*
> *she entered our room and lay down*
> *next to me, her hand resting on*
> *my chest, her breath mixing with mine.*
> *I wanted to fight her, tell her*
> *she could not replace you, but she*
> *smiled and climbed atop my hungry body.*

MY FACE IS STILL DAMP from the fever of my dream. I release the pen from my hand and step away from the desk in my home office. I am ashamed that I still feel the stiffness of my erection, as if I have done something wrong in subconsciously exploring another woman.

I sit on the recliner in the den, trying to shake my thoughts, but the sun rises on me, illuminating my guilt.

THE CLOCK READS ten o'clock at night, and I have

barely moved twenty-five feet all day. Now I sit at the computer in my office, checking the e-mail on my school account. I find a schedule sent out by the provost outlining the faculty workshops that will start next week. Ellison-Wright College typically schedules their pre-school faculty meetings to coincide with Freshmen Week so the students will have access to everyone who will be teaching throughout the semester. It usually requires a lot of sitting around in the office waiting for kids who never show up. But at least now the schedule has officially been sent out.

As I close out my e-mail account, I hear the chiming sound of WEB Instant Messenger. Marcus is three hours behind in time, so this is the perfect time for us to catch up. When I click the box on my laptop, I don't see Marcus's handle, Mr. Marcus, not to be confused with, uh, the *other* Mr. Marcus, porn star extraordinaire. I don't even recognize the name on the screen. The message simply reads "Hey" and it comes from a person with the handle "Coco404."

"Hey," I type.

"How have you been, Dr. Nelson?"

I laugh. Tanya has actually reached out to me. Suddenly my stomach tightens as I try to steel my nerves. It wouldn't be wise of me to read anything into her instant messaging me, would it?

"Things on this ends are better. Just got the faculty schedule for next week."

"Excited?"

"Not really."

"Sorry I'm just now getting at you."

My eyebrow lifts involuntarily. "That's all right."

"Why aren't you out tonight?" she types.

"I should be asking you the same thing."

"I like chillin' out on the weekends."

"I can understand that."

"Can I ask you a question?"

I pause and take a deep breath. "Sure."

"What have you been doing to pass the time?"

My face scrunches up in confusion. "Pass the time *how*?"

She hesitates for a moment before typing, "My father left my mom and me when I was seventeen. We took it pretty hard. We had to find our own ways of getting back into the flow." She pauses and then continues typing. "I just wanted to know if you've been taking good care of yourself."

I stare at the screen wondering why any of what I feel even matters to this woman, this *girl*. I reread her comment again and realize that she is just being genuine, so I answer, "I haven't really done much of anything, other than writing and going to the bookstore. It's all still strange to me."

"I feel you."

"Really?"

"Yeah. Is there anything I could do to help out?"

"What do you mean?"

"You know. Like have you had a home-cooked meal lately? That kind of thing."

I chuckle under my breath. I type, "So you cook?"

"I do a little somethin' somethin'."

"What do you cook?" I ask, playing along.

"Fried chicken, macaroni and cheese, collard greens, cornbread, peach cobbler, all of that stuff."

My stomach starts to growl, and the rumbling sensation forces me to sober up. "You'd cook all of that for me?"

"Yeah. Why not? You're cool people."

"So you're going to bring me a plate when school starts?"

"I can bring it to your house before that, if you want."

I stare at the screen and stand up from my computer. I look toward the kitchen, noticing the fast food bags strewn across the counter, knowing that the refrigerator only has water, apple juice, and old condiments. I sit down and begin typing. "When?"

"This weekend, if that's cool."

"OK."

"That's what's up. *BRB.*"

I stare at the abbreviation for "be right back," which my brother uses often. When she returns, she asks for my address, and I give it to her, still feeling uneasy about the nature of it all.

"What time?" she types.

"Any time is fine."

"I have to go to a sorority meeting Saturday afternoon, but I can bring it over later. Say seven or so?"

"That's fine," I type. "But can I ask you a question?"

"Sure."

Slowly I type the word "why" and push send.

She responds almost immediately. "Because you seem like you could use it."

## CHAPTER EIGHT

"WHOA!" IS ALL MARCUS CAN MUSTER AS I TELL him about Tanya's offer to cook me dinner.

The whole situation makes me feel uncomfortable, and Marcus is the only one whose advice I can trust. Calling him was a no-brainer.

"Is there a rule against faculty and students hookin' up?" he asks.

"Not officially, but it's kind of an unwritten rule that you're not supposed to do it."

"But is she *fine?*"

That's my brother for you, always sizing up the aesthetics first.

"She's pretty, but this whole thing doesn't feel right."

"Give me one reason why it's wrong," Marcus pushes me.

"She's half my age."

"Shit. Give me another."

"She's a student."

"Give me another.

"It's still too soon."

He sighs. "OK. Let me break it down for you, little brother. Age is relative. Maturity is how you should gauge compatibility. Second, if it ain't written down, you can always fake like you didn't know that shit. And third, you're not looking to fall in love. You just want some companionship. That's normal, especially when you're lonely. And it's healthy to be around someone who can make you smile. Nobody would hold that against you, so you don't need to hold it against yourself."

Everything he is telling me makes sense, but it doesn't put me any closer to feeling at ease. "Maybe I'm jumping the gun here. Maybe it *is* just a meal."

"The girl likes you."

"How do you know?" I ask, wanting desperately to understand my brother's insight.

"Everything you've told me. Just the initiative she's taken suggests something."

"But why?"

"Damned if I know," he says, laughing. "No, seriously, dude, you're a nice looking guy, you take care of yourself, you're intelligent, and you're a good person. Hell, if you spent any time outside of your house, you'd have heard that shit from a million women by now."

I laugh. He's my brother. He's supposed to make me feel better about myself.

"So I should go ahead with the dinner?"

"Definitely. And then call me when it's over and let me know how everything went down."

"Well, I appreciate your help."

"No problem."

I prepare to hang up.

"Ed?"

"Yes," I say, catching his voice just in time.

"Do me a favor and just relax. Try to enjoy yourself. That's all you want at this point anyway."

"Sure," I respond, more because I know that's what he wants to hear.

Placing the phone back into my pocket, I pull back the curtain on my window and stare at the full moon of a Friday night.

# CHAPTER NINE

Straightening the house on Saturday morning, I find myself bubbling with nervousness. There is not much to clean, just taking out the garbage, vacuuming, and straightening the furniture. I open the drapes and tie them, allowing the sunlight to sweep throughout the den. Everything looks presentable, and that's when my eye catches the only photograph of my wife in the room.

The guilt starts to work on me again. Although it's been over three months since my wife passed away, I haven't been intimate in over a year and a half. The radiation and chemo took such a toll on her body that she never felt well enough for us to have sex. Dealing with that situation didn't do much to stimulate my sex drive either. Other than a few rushed moments alone in the shower, I had managed to make it all this time with very little sexual release. That's why the dream I had the other night scared me. The erection was real, as was the conversation the following night. Everything in my mind wants to keep my thoughts about Tanya pure and platonic, but my body is clearly screaming for much more. The whole thing is dizzying, and I shake my head, angry at myself for having these thoughts in front of Charlotte's photograph.

I stand there for a moment contemplating whether or not to put the picture frame in the room or let it remain in its current place. I don't know how it will make me feel to have it there, especially with the open nature of Tanya's visit. It feels as though I am being devious by even considering taking it down.

And I feel like a complete traitor when I actually take the photograph back to the master bedroom, a place I consider off-limits, and put it on the dresser. As I return to the den, I wonder if I'm assuming too much about Tanya or if I'm underestimating her entirely.

---

THE SUN HAS BEGUN to set, but it is still very bright outside when I see Tanya's small blue Ford Focus pull into the driveway. I walk outside to help her carry the containers sitting across the backseat. Taking an armful of Tupperware containers out of the car, I glance around and relish the fact that I live in a small, quiet neighborhood with neighbors who don't care what happens at my house, as long as it does not adversely affect their own property values. I escort Tanya into the house, unable to remove my eyes from her long, toned legs coming out from under her denim shorts, her blue sorority shirt resting loosely atop her sculpted bottom. I try not to stare, as we place everything on the kitchen table.

The smell of the fried chicken is even more intense now. My mouth begins to water, and I can't even see the actual food yet. I take two plates out of the cupboard and start removing lids.

"Oh, I can't stay," she says. "I was just dropping everything off."

"But there's so much food. You'll have to help me out here," I respond, making light of the fact that she had just floored me with her comment.

"No, this is all for you—so you'll have some good food to eat throughout the week."

"None for the cook?" I say, playfully lifting the fried chicken for her to see.

"My boyfriend is supposed to be taking me out to eat tonight, so I'm going to have to pass. Maybe next time."

I nod, conscious of ever muscle in my lips that could betray me and reveal my growing disappointment.

"Well, I appreciate the food. It smells wonderful!"

"Thank you," she responds, her keys still dangling from her hand.

I wonder if we will chat later online. Probably not.

"I can give you back your containers," I offer.

"Naw, that's OK. I don't need them. I have more than enough."

She leans on the door, and I follow her out into the driveway.

"Well, thank you for everything," I say, watching her step into her car.

"No problem. I just hope you enjoy it."

"I'm sure I will."

She pulls out of the driveway, back onto the street, and just like that, she's gone.

Walking into the house, I feel like the biggest fool known to man, and as much as I want to fix a plate of her good home cooking, I shake my head in complete confusion, realizing that what I really wanted for dinner was her.

## CHAPTER TEN

ONCE, WHILE IN GRAD SCHOOL, ONE OF MY literature professors spent a week breaking down David Mamet's play *Oleanna*, the story of a university professor who finds himself defending his career against charges of sexual harassment by a female student, nothing to sneeze at for a professor seeking tenure. The beauty of the play, according to my professor, was that the facts could be interpreted in two very different ways, giving rise to the plausibility that both characters were correct in what took place. The only problem with this *Doubt*-like approach to drama is that it allows the reader to plug in his or her own personal biases into making sense of what really happens.

Now I wonder if I have done anything that has put me into the same boat as Mamet's character. Over and over I replay everything from our conversation at JoAnne's Books and Java to the instant messaging. I even replay everything I said to her while she was here. Had I stepped out too far? I didn't think I had, but I couldn't be sure.

The fact that she had conveniently failed to mention she had a boyfriend struck me as odd at first. Now, I realize the topic had just never come up. If she had no problem talking about it to my face, then she wasn't intentionally hiding it from me in our earlier conversations. I had just seen what I wanted to see.

"Oh lord. I'm that creepy old man who likes girls half his age," I think to myself, embarrassed and ashamed by the revelation.

I pick up my cell phone to call Marcus. I get his voicemail and hang up.

Opening my laptop, I pull up a new Word document and stare at the blinking cursor, hoping to write myself right. Nothing comes out of me, and every letter I type, I quickly delete. Feeling the weight of the day upon my shoulders, I walk back into the bedroom, where I see Charlotte's picture gazing at me from its pewter frame. Just then I am struck with words, so I find my pen and quickly scribble a poem on the notepad resting on my nightstand:

*No. 22*

> *I push her away, but she returns*
> *To me when the lights are low*
> *And flames ripple across these cold walls.*
> *I want to savor the taste of*
> *Her…and know the urgency of now,*
> *But I am still haunted by the*
> *Bitter/sweet taste of our last kiss.*

I TURN off the light and lie down atop the sheets and stare at the ceiling, wanting only to understand why it's the loneliness part of being alone that sucks so much.

# CHAPTER ELEVEN

I WAKE EARLY SUNDAY MORNING AND TURN ON A little Frankie Beverly and Maze, while I do my morning pushups and sit-ups. The sun has lit up my den like a Christmas tree, reminding me of the fact that the drapes are still tied back. Stretching, I find myself singing along with "We Are One."

"I can't understand why we treat each other in this way," I sing, enjoying a little two-step dance move. I mumble through the rest of the words until I get to the chorus. "We are one." Yeah, that's my song.

I brush my teeth and toss on a pair of jeans and a polo shirt. I have no destination, but I feel, at the very least, I will go for a drive, just to get some fresh air. I grab a breakfast bar and a glass of orange juice and take a seat at the computer in my office to read the morning news, a habit I developed when I found myself unable to keep up with the growing mound of news "paper" that accumulated while I took care of my wife. Now I have my morning news reading down to a science, and I don't have to worry about driving to a recycling center every few months.

I click the mouse, waking up my computer screen. A message box is sitting in the center of the screen from Coco404. It arrived shortly after midnight last night. It reads, "I hope you enjoyed your dinner. "

It's at this moment that I confess to myself I have no idea of how I should read any of her comments anymore.

---

ONE OF MY favorite things to do is drive up to the Druid Hills exit on I-85 and swing around, coming south back into the downtown area. Atlanta has a small, yet beautiful, skyline, its buildings glistening in the bright, clear August morning sun. For all of sixty seconds, you can take in this aesthetic scene before going under an overpass and pushing out toward the I-20 exits. This one little stretch of highway is the only reason I bother with the interstate at all, because any local will tell you that there are several routes to and from a place, just to avoid the gridlock of rush hour traffic.

Charlotte used to love taking Sunday morning drives. It was the one time we could move in peace up and down the highways. We would grab lunch from a small family-run Italian restaurant downtown on Ponce de Leon and eat out on the patio beneath a huge burgundy umbrella, while we watched the most dedicated of joggers pass us by. It was a part of our new life, since the passing of our son, as we embraced the notion we were in fact a strong family unit, just the two of us.

Before we moved to Atlanta, we lived two years in the northeastern part of Mississippi in a town called Saltillo, an area right outside of Tupelo. We had been there for four months when we learned we would be having a child. I still remember Charlotte's smile and the way we held each other when she showed me the pregnancy test. She took two more, just to be sure, before we met with an obstetrician. We both read *What to Expect When Expecting*, and I attended classes with her so I could learn to better support her during the birthing process. We did everything by the book and enjoyed a bountiful baby shower that would have taken us well past the first twelve months with gifts.

There was not a single sign that the pregnancy would end so badly. Standing there, holding Charlotte's hand while she screamed and pushed, I could only vaguely make out the doctor saying something about the umbilical cord being wrapped around my son's neck. It was only after my doctor held up my lifeless son and tried to revive him that I realized my life would never be the same.

We left Mississippi at the end of that school year, and I took a job with Ellison-Wright College, a prestigious historically black college with a campus of three thousand students. Day-by-day, week-by-week, Charlotte and I worked to reconstruct our life, to heal ourselves. I would like to believe that we succeeded in doing just that.

Now I am alone, feeling the weight of having had to bury both my son and my wife. I remember when Charlotte and I first arrived in Atlanta and we made a promise to each other to live life to the fullest.

It's that very promise that allows me to wake up each morning, open to the infinite possibilities of life, rather than just wither up and die.

# CHAPTER TWELVE

---

After spending most of the day driving around the Atlanta metro area, I am anxious to warm up some of the fried chicken and other side dishes that Tanya brought over last night. I must admit that while I was disappointed that things did not turn out the way I had hoped, the dinner she left me was better than anything I had eaten in quite some time.

I make my plate and take it over to the computer so that I can surf the Internet while I eat. Tanya's message is still there from earlier. I type, "I'm enjoying your cooking now " and open my browser to start checking my bookmarked news sites. I take a bite of the collard greens and cornbread and close my eyes. This is a damn shame, having access to someone who can throw down like this!

I enjoy my meal and set the empty plate off to the side. The sun is now setting, and I know I will need to get ready for bed soon, especially with the faculty meetings starting at nine o'clock the next morning. The chime on my computer rings, and I see that I have a message from Coco404. It reads, "I'm glad you liked it."

"I think I'm going to sleep well tonight. Full stomach."

"LOL! That's what's up."

"Wish you could have joined me," I type, before realizing what I have just done.

"I should have."

I read her reply several times before responding, "Dinner didn't go well?"

"No. I'm too through with him."

"What happened?"

"I'm sick of running into his ex-girlfriends everywhere we go. I know he's messing around."

"Are they coming up to you or something?" I ask.

It begins to dawn on me that I am now on the verge of giving advice to her about her own relationship, a situation that makes very little sense, given everything else that's happened up to this point.

"I almost had to whip this one chick's ass last night. Eyeing him like I'm not even there. And he didn't do shit! Just flat-out disrespected me!"

"That's his loss," I type.

"I don't know," she continues. "I'm just tired. I'm not so desperate I gotta just take shit off this Negro."

I nod, but before I can type my response, she types, "Sorry for my language."

"Don't apologize. Sometimes you have to just use the words you feel."

A minute passes before she sends me another message.

"You're pretty cool, Dr. Nelson."

It's at this moment that I realize I am about to alter the dynamics of our discussion, but it feels too uncomfortable for us to maintain these formalities, especially when she's confiding in me like this.

"Just call me Ed."

Another pause on her end.

"So what did you do today, Ed?"

"Go for a drive—and enjoy a very delicious meal ."

"How much do you have left?"

"About two pieces of chicken. A little bit of every-thing else. Maybe enough to get through Tuesday."

"Need me to make you another plate?"

I smile. "I couldn't put you through all of that trouble again."

"It's no trouble. Trust. A sista's gotta eat too."

"Well, then yes—but only if you'll join me for dinner."

Another pause, this one much longer than the first.

"OK. When do you want to do it?"

The phrasing of her words starts to tap into my subconscious, causing me to lean over, adjusting the pressure building between my legs.

"How is next weekend?"

"The frats are throwing a back-to-school pajama jam next Friday. Saturday looks good, though."

"Seven again?"

"That'll work."

I glance at the clock on my computer screen. It's late and I know I need to lie down and get some sleep so I can deal with the long, tiring workshops tomor-row. Part of me wants to stay online, just to be con-nected to someone who actually wants to talk to me—someone who is not my brother.

"I have to get up early," I type reluctantly. "Will talk to you later."

She responds, "Cool. Have sweet dreams, Ed."

"You too."

I stand up from the computer, my stomach bub-bling with butterflies. I try not to overthink all of this. Just be open to the experience, I remind myself.

# CHAPTER THIRTEEN

THE FACULTY RETREAT AT ELLISON-WRIGHT College is widely regarded as a waste of time beyond the opening two-hour session, where the president of the college updates us with the recent administrative changes and sets forth the goals of the school year. Everything else is a series of fruitless workshops, normally conducted by faculty members who had to forfeit part of their vacation breaks to prepare dull PowerPoint presentations for apathetic colleagues.

This year is no different, and by the time we break for lunch, I want only to return to my office, a place I haven't spent much time in since December of the previous year, and get re-acclimated to being on campus. Walking back toward my building, a few of my colleagues from the School of Liberal Arts walk up to me, patting me on my back to express their condolences for my wife. None of them attended the funeral, but today all of them want to feel like they are supporting me. It doesn't faze me though. The politics of academia are like lying down with snakes: it's OK, as long as you know where the heads are while you sleep.

My office is a small cubbyhole at the end of a narrow, cluttered hall. When I open the door, I am immediately met with the stale smell of books that have lain dormant for too long. The first thing I do is crack open the windows on the two walls that form the corner where my desk sits. Charlotte's face smiles at me from a 4 x 6 inch frame on my desk. This will be the first year of my teaching without her being a phone call away.

"It's good to see you back, Dr. Nelson," I hear from my doorway.

I look up to find the department secretary, Missy Alexander. Missy has been with us in the African-American Studies department for three years now, having taken the job right after she graduated from Ellison-Wright. The irony is that she never took a class in our department while she was a student, but seems to know the ins and outs of our department policies and programs better than most of the professors who teach here.

I smile and nod my thanks to her.

"If you need anything, just let me know."

"Thank you," I say, taking a seat behind my desk and turning on what appears to be a new computer monitor and tower situated at the edge of my desk. Relief washes over me because my computer from the previous year was so old and sluggish I had to use my personal laptop from home. Now it seems that I can forgo the added weight of a computer bag and just rely on this new setup. It's always the small things that keep employees happy, and that seems to be the one thing Ellison-Wright is good at.

I reach in my satchel and remove a small Tupperware container of fried chicken, macaroni and cheese, and what's left of the collard greens. I take the container over to the microwave that sits on a small table in the corner opposite my desk. As I wait for the microwave to chime that my food is ready, I visualize seeing Tanya on Saturday. I wonder what she will be wearing. I wonder what I should wear.

I wonder again if I am overthinking everything.

Taking the container back to my desk, I enjoy my meal in the peaceful silence of my office, totally oblivious to the pending workshops that will fill the rest of the day.

---

ON MY WAY across campus to the next workshop, I can vaguely make out Tanya walking in the distance. I fix my eyes to focus better, trying to avoid the impression that I am staring. She is wearing an orange and yellow sundress, revealing the smooth brown skin of her shoulders, and a pair of dark sunglasses, but the hair and complexion are a dead giveaway. She looks in my direction, and I wonder if she sees me. Her lips spread into a smile, and she waves her hand subtly at me. I begin to walk in her direction, as she approaches me.

Extending her arms, she embraces me like a friend she has not seen since the spring semester ended. I welcome the soft feel of her body pressed against mine.

"Hi, Dr. Nelson," she says, a slight smirk on her face.

"Hi, Tanya."

"How does it feel to be back?"

"Same old, same old."

"It'll be a good year," she insists.

"Yeah, that's what I'm hoping."

She glances over my shoulder, and I angle my head to see other professors moving slowly across campus, like cattle being herded across a field.

"I guess I should get back to my workshops."

She smiles. "Yeah. I have to run over to the administration building to check on the stipend for my scholarship."

"Well, I guess I'll catch up with you later," I say.

"You gonna be online tonight?"

"Probably so."

"Cool," she responds, touching my arm and turning to walk toward the administration building.

I watch her hips sway sweetly beneath the thin fabric of her sundress.

Walking toward my next workshop location, I feel as though I am keeping a secret from everyone. The only relief I have is knowing that everyone sees me as the grieving husband, a status that I prefer because people tend to respect your space out of fear of being sucked into your perceived depression.

Yes, it is better to be left alone, than for people to gossip about any growing infatuation I might possibly have with one of our students.

# CHAPTER FOURTEEN

"SHE'S ALL IN YOUR HEAD," MARCUS SAYS, excitement growing in his voice. "She's got your mind all fucked up. Got you all discombobulated and shit!"

My brother loves to mix curse words with SAT words. That is his way of openly defying the old adage that people only curse because they lack the proper vocabularies to express themselves.

"You've been had. You've been hoodwinked. Bamboozled," he continues, invoking Spike Lee's famous Malcolm X scene. "Little brother, don't be pussy whipped! Reverse that shit, and whip that pussy!"

When my brother is on a roll with movie lines, he's on a roll.

"Wouldn't that require that I am at least intimate with her?" I respond, playing along with him, as I steer my Jeep Liberty onto I-20.

I hear him "tsk-tsking" into the microphone of his cell phone.

"That ham is cooked, glazed, and ready to be sliced!" he says, now breathless from his exertions.

"Are you out of movie lines yet?" I ask. "Because I really do need some advice here."

I am grateful that the traffic is moving and holding out hope that I will not get stuck in bumper-to-bumper traffic when I exit onto I-85 South. But if I do, Marcus can always say the right thing to make the trip more bearable.

"OK," he starts. "Let's run down the facts. First, she volunteers to cook for you—and does it. Then, she tells you about her 'boyfriend,' but still chats online with you, spilling their business to you. And then finally, she agrees to meet with you—again—and have dinner, this time with no confusion whatsoever. Dude, come on! She's running game on you. She wants to make sure you're really feeling her before she puts herself out there."

"Interesting theory, but I was wrong before when I assumed too much," I say.

"Ed, you got that wrong. You didn't assume *too much*. You just assumed, which is a human instinct, steeped in survival. You assume the chair will not fall out from under you. You assume a plane will stay in the air. We all assume shit. That's natural. Sure, sometimes shit doesn't happen the way we expect, but does that stop us from using our God-given faculties to make sense of this thing called 'life' anyway? Hell no! And when it comes to ole girl, we're gonna keep on using our best judgment and assuming our asses off."

I smile. I don't know whether I buy everything he's saying, but I do believe that, regardless of what happens, my mind will continue to try to make sense of things.

"OK," I say finally. "I see where you're coming from."

"Seriously, you don't have to stress this shit. What's gonna be is gonna be. Either she tips her hand or you just jack your shit off before you go to sleep."

I laugh, slapping my steering wheel. "Man, you're cracking me up!"

"Don't play. If she gets you stiff and nothing jumps off, you just *handle* that shit, if you catch my drift."

Only my brother could recommend masturbation as a way of overcoming confusion, but standing from his perch on the penthouse ledge of bachelordom, I'm in no position to argue with his advice. I'm just hopeful that I'll at least have choices.

I-85 is clear as I cruise down toward the Union City exit. The sky is wide and clear, the kind of sky that rings with opportunity—yet the same sky that saw me sleeping off my intoxication months earlier, curled against a tombstone with a bottle of Johnnie Walker.

## CHAPTER FIFTEEN

My house is probably the most nondescript house in my Fairburn subdivision, and that's probably one of the things that attracted Charlotte initially. I had hoped we would find a nice home off of Cascade Road, just outside of southwest Atlanta, an area affectionately referred to as "The Swats" by my students. A house in that area would have meant a commute of less than ten minutes, without the need to hop on the interstate. Charlotte needed something a bit more familiar, however, something that looked, or at least felt, like the small town she had grown up in. Fairburn was a city that seemed to comfortably meet that definition, close enough to Atlanta, but with a small town feel.

Five years we spent making this house into a home, and there is not a single inch of space that does not contain some memory of her. We made love on nearly every piece of furniture that we own, including counters, walls, and other fixtures built into the house. There were thousands of kisses in the foyer, the kitchen, the bathroom, the hallways. There was not one inch of space that did not swell with the wonderful sensation of her voice bouncing off the walls.

This house was truly my wife's home.

Now I wrestle with what it means to bring another woman into this space. It wasn't like I didn't consider it last Saturday, but for some reason the idea has taken root much deeper, as I have lost myself in these fantasies of Tanya. I tell myself that I am not a traitor, that what I am thinking is natural, but I don't know if I'm lying to myself because I feel the heat of lust breathing down my neck.

I wonder at what point does what was ours become what is mine: the couch, the king-sized bed with its huge mahogany sleigh-bed frame, the large jet-stream bath—all things that we have christened with our love. At what point can another woman recline or sleep or bathe here? I don't want to leave my home for some neutral, nameless place with no character, because I love what this place represents. But at the same time, I don't want to desecrate my wife's memory.

Even if it is not Tanya and it ends up being another woman a year from now, I need to know how I will deal with this. The only thing tugging at my heart is a set of memories that can never leave. I am not concerned with what other people think of me. I want only to feel as if I can live again, without that looming shadow of guilt whispering to me from the corners of this house.

---

I AM LOGGED onto my computer for nearly three hours surfing the Internet before the chime of my WEB instant messaging account sounds out. I had been eagerly anticipating the sound, but now that it is here I feel the familiar bubbling of nerves in my stomach.

"How r u?" it reads.

"Fine. Just messing around on the net. You?"

"Taking a break."

"From what?" I ask.

"Everything."

"Are you OK?"

"Not really."

"What's wrong?"

"Don't want to bore you with my problems."

I stare at the screen for a moment, my fingers resting on the keys. I ponder just how much I want to be a part of what is bothering her. The logical thing is to ask, but getting involved in her personal life requires an investment beyond merely fantasizing about her.

I inquire, in spite of myself.

She begins to talk about her boyfriend, who it turns out is not a student at Ellison-Wright, but a cook at Jean-Louis. Every detail she discloses takes me deeper into her frustrations with her life: her suspicions of her boyfriend having gotten a woman from Columbus pregnant, her wanting to find another job because of the whispering and embarrassment about her relationship at work, and the fact that she is still heavily conflicted about her father leaving. It's a lot to share with a person she barely knows, but I give her the ear she needs, allowing her the space to vent.

I can't see her tears, but I can feel them, and I want only to tell her things will get better and that she can do much better than her boyfriend, but it's not my place to give that kind of advice. That seems like something one of her girlfriends would bring up. Instead, I tell her how many wonderful things she has working in her favor: intelligence, maturity, accountability, tenacity, beauty, and, to lighten the mood, wonderful cooking skills.

"LOL!" she types.

I smile.

"I know everything is gonna get better. And I know

I need to get rid of Kevin. It's just that sometimes everything stacks up on me all at once."

"I understand," I respond.

"I have other things I need to focus on anyway—like this party."

"Tell me about the party," I type, hoping to push her mind toward something less stressful.

"We're hosting a pajama jam with the frats this Friday."

"I remember you mentioning that last time," I offer, wondering if it will be anything like the sexy romps we used to have back when I was in college, where the girls wore teddies and the guys wore silk boxers, all while dancing as close to each other as possible.

"Yeah. We all put on sleepwear and party. It's one of our biggest fundraisers of the year and a good way to get a rep as the best party throwers on campus."

"We used to do the same thing back when I was in school."

"For real? You were a boxer guy, weren't you?"

I smile. "What makes you say that?"

"You just look like the boxer type," she responds.

"And what does the 'boxer' type look like?"

"You know. An athletic guy. Larger, stronger guy who likes a looser fit."

Was she talking about me? I never thought of myself the way she was describing me, simply because I haven't looked at myself in that sense in several years. I just knew that Charlotte liked me the way I was, and as far as I was concerned, I didn't have to dig any deeper than that. I lift my arm and make a muscle, laughing to myself. So *that's* the way she sees me.

"Interesting," I type.

":-)."

"So have you picked out your pajamas for the party yet?"

The question just falls out there, natural as the conversation.

"Yeah. It's nice. Wanna see it?"

"Sure," I type.

"You have a webcam?"

"Yes."

"BRB."

I look up at the clock located at the top of my desktop. It's 10:30, but it feels much later with all of the lights turned off in my house, except the light coming from my laptop. It feels as if my existence right now is totally virtual, as if turning off my computer would send me flailing through an abyss of blackness.

My WEB instant messenger client signals Co-co404's desire to engage in video conferencing, and I click the "Accept" button. Within seconds, I see a video display of Tanya's face, with a small screen of myself from my webcam in the upper corner.

"Hey, can you hear me?" she asks, her face inches from the screen. Her voice is clear and surprisingly loud in the silent space of my house.

"Yes. Can you hear *me*?"

"Yeah," she says, giggling.

"Ready?" she asks.

"Sure. "

I don't know why I expect her to hold up her outfit on a hanger, the same way I would see it in a store, but she simply stands up, revealing a cream colored slip that complements her rich chocolate brown skin tone. Her bare arms are toned as the spaghetti straps on each side rest gently on her shoulders. I can see her thighs extending from beneath the slip, and I swear I can make out the shape of her nipples through the thin fabric.

"What do you think?" she asks.

"I can't really see everything," I respond, clearly lying.

She steps back a little farther from the camera so that I can take in the full view of her toned body as the satin fabric falls seductively upon her curves. She poses, as if modeling, and turns around so that I can get a view of her backside. To put it mildly, she looks incredibly sexy.

She walks back to her computer, taking a seat so that only her upper body is visible in the frame. "So?" she asks, a smile dancing across her face.

Even if I ventured to downplay her showcase a number of different ways, my lie would still be equally obvious each time. I can only muster, "Nice."

"You know what, Ed? You're cool people," she says, her words starting to take on an echo-like effect from our previous conversations.

I chuckle lightly under my breath. My mind is now dancing with thoughts of her body, and I want only to see her once again, posing in front of the camera. I feel the butterflies flooding my body as I realize I am about to push the envelope a little further.

"Can I see your lingerie again?"

I watch as she ponders my request and responds, "Why?"

The word rings out in the silence of my house, and I realize I have no explanation other than the fact that I feel a burning desire to gaze upon her body again. I want to answer her, but I can't find anything diplomatic to say to justify my request.

"You're feeling me, aren't you?" she asks, her innocence disguising her ability to read me as plain as day.

This is the moment I have been anticipating, the moment where we stop playing games and really start to communicate. I can't feel the firmness of the floor beneath my feet, just the uncomfortable feeling of being suspended in mid-air, held there by her gaze.

I look down, trying to suppress a nervous smile.

"It's cool," she says, prompting me. "I'm not gonna say anything to anyone."

I lift my head. "Yes."

She smiles. "You know you didn't have to draw it all out. You could've just said something."

"Like what?" I ask, my tone light and somewhat relieved.

"You could've been like, 'Tanya, you are so sexy. You got it goin' on,'" she says, laughing.

"Oh, so it was that simple?" I joke, playing along.

"Yeah. Just be straight up. Girls like that."

I nod. "Since we're being straight up, I want to know if you're feeling me, too?"

She looks me up and down on the display on her computer. "You a'ight," she says, chuckling. "I'm not complaining."

I no longer try to conceal my smile. My stomach is dancing.

"So, my question still stands," I say.

"What question?"

"Can I see your night gown again?"

She lifts her eyes as if to consider my request. "I guess so," she responds, in mock reluctance.

She stands up and begins to dance, her body moving rhythmically to a melody that only we can hear. I watch the way her hips roll, the way her arms stretch upward as she sways her body. She places her hands on her hair as she moves, her eyes closed. She opens them slowly, as if waking from a dream, and struts toward her computer.

"That's all for tonight, Ed," she says coyly.

My erection is so strong I shift uncomfortably from the aching tension in my pants. I want her so badly that I will do anything.

"So I will see you on Saturday?" I ask, not even worrying about how thirsty I might appear at the moment.

"That's the plan, isn't it," she responds.

"Yes."

"Then, I'll see you on Saturday."

I nod. "OK."

Coco404 disconnects the webcam and goes offline. With thoughts of her still dancing in my mind, I close my laptop and embrace the darkness that surrounds me.

# CHAPTER SIXTEEN

THUMBING THROUGH MAIL WHILE SITTING IN MY office, I come across a photocopied article that had been placed in my department mailbox. My name is printed across the top of the front page, and I would have set it to the side, had I not seen my name appear randomly throughout the first page. "What Nelson fails to see," "such naivety from an academician is inexcusable," "maybe Nelson's intention is to have black people be a godless people, in spite of thousands of years to the contrary": all quotes in this paper. The paper does not strike me as being particularly academic in nature, but its author has managed to find some obscure journal willing to publish it. I look at the by-line and see the name: Rev. Dr. Cordell Murphy, an up-and-coming professor in Ellison-Wright's religion department.

I stare at the paper for a moment, flabbergasted that another faculty member would so publicly attack me. I have had more than a few disagreements over the years with my colleagues, but I have never taken my thoughts public in so unprofessional a way. My first thought is to walk over to the religion department across campus and kick Cordell's ass, but I quickly sit back in my chair and breathe, the one thing that seems to slow me down when I get upset.

Nearly a year ago, I had written a paper that got published in a journal on African-American studies. The paper tied into some research I had been conducting as an offshoot of my dissertation on present day vestiges of transatlantic slavery. This particular paper dealt with religion as one of those vestiges—not the most revolutionary of ideas, I must admit, but it seemed to fit in perfectly with the debate surrounding Rev. Jeremiah Wright during President's Obama's first presidential campaign. Although I never mentioned Rev. Wright, or President Obama's pluralist upbringing for that matter, I did refer to my curiosity at the growing religious conservatism of black people, given that religious conservatism was often a significant justification for their own historical persecution by racist whites. I knew the paper would be the subject of debate, as anything that involves religion tends to be, but I was hoping to temper some of that reaction by focusing exclusively on the subject from a historical perspective. Apparently, Cordell took offense to my paper and decided to take me to task as publicly as he could.

I place the paper on my desk and shake my head. He is citing my paper, citing my *facts*, and countering with pure theological and hermeneutical subjectivity. I should be glad that my paper has even stimulated this degree of debate. After all, the paper was designed primarily to strengthen my CV for tenure review by putting a few more publications under my belt. I shouldn't be mad at Cordell. In fact, I should be thanking him, I tell myself. Just off of my response to his counter-argument, I can secure another publication credit before the end of the school year—that is if anyone even cares about this discussion at all.

I lean back in my chair and look out the window,

over the quad. Next week students will be walking back and forth across this campus like ants swarming a kicked anthill. Tanya will be among those students, and I wonder briefly if I will even be able to make her out from my office window as she goes about her daily activities.

My daydreaming is interrupted by a knock on my door. I look up to see the chair of my department, Dr. Evelyn Chambers. "Got a minute?" she asks.

"Sure."

She walks into my office and leans against the file cabinet pushed against the wall by the door. "I just wanted to welcome you back and let you know that if you need anything, we're here for you."

"Thank you."

She glances around my office before continuing, "I also wanted to let you know that the dean has appointed you to serve on the presidential scholarship committee. You will serve as the representative for the School of Liberal Arts. I hope that's not a problem. Don't worry. They only meet once each semester to review scholarships that were awarded the previous semester to ensure grade point averages are maintained and all of that jazz."

"No problem." I know I will have to probably serve on a few more committees before the year is out. The good thing about serving on a committee that rarely meets is that you get credit for the committee on your CV without the time burdens often associated with most school committees.

"Good. The dean just notified me that you will be meeting later this afternoon at four o'clock in the Hughes Hall conference room. Will you be able to make it?"

One of the things that I don't miss about Ellison-Wright is their need to spring things on you at the last minute. But being that classes have not started and the fact that my syllabi have already been submitted to the copy center, my schedule is actually open.

"Sure. No problem," I say.

She smiles and pulls the door closed behind her as she leaves.

One day, when I get tenure, I will be in that magnanimous position to use the magic word that most professors here dare use, and use it without fear of repercussion. A simple word, only two letters, but it embodies the essence of freedom: no.

---

THE GODS MUST SURELY HAVE a sense of humor, because the eight person committee that oversees the presidential scholarship reviews for Ellison-Wright includes the one person I would have loved to avoid altogether: Cordell Murphy. He sits smugly down the table from me, as if through his article, he has attained some kind of moral superiority over me. I ignore him and focus my eyes on the list of scholarship recipients being handed around the table.

Excluding grants and private scholarships, Ellison-Wright gives out ten different full academic scholarships, known as presidential scholarships, each year. They are renewable each year if the recipient maintains a 3.0 GPA or better for both the fall and spring semesters. I look at the names on the list, and oddly, I don't recognize any of them. The scholarship recipients all have GPAs that are well into the 3.0 – 4.0 range.

The meeting goes by quickly, and we plan to meet again in January before the spring semester begins. But rather than return to my office, I go home and take a nap.

Saturday is right around the corner, and the upcoming dinner feels like a loaded nine-millimeter in my virgin hands. Its beauty is chilling, but I cannot afford to forget its inherent danger.

# CHAPTER SEVENTEEN

---

*No. 25*

*I carry her smile home with me,*
*my fingers locked around this Pandora's box,*
*eager to place it atop my desk*
*and unleash that wicked light into this*
*space that yearns to feel the heat*
*that dances from her sweet lips, calling*
*my heart to ignite what's left inside.*

## CHAPTER EIGHTEEN

MY HOUSE IS SO CLEAN THAT IT LOOKS LIKE THE showcase house for a start-up subdivision. I have not seen it this clean in quite a while. In fact, I woke up early this morning vacuuming, dusting, sweeping, and putting things away. It's Saturday, and while Tanya won't be here until around seven, I feel as though I need to be preparing for her, which is ironic since she is the one who is cooking tonight's dinner.

Satisfied with the cleanliness of the house, I toss on a t-shirt and some sweatpants and head over to the gym for a quick workout. My mind flows in a million different directions as I jog on the treadmill with Ledisi's "Alright" playing in the ear buds of my iPod. The energy pulsing through my legs feels good, and my breaths are matching the drop of each foot. "Everything is everything; it's gonna be alright," I find myself singing under my breath. I smile as sweat trickles down the side of my face and my abs tense with the movement of my legs. After my cool down, I do some benching, back work, curls, and triceps pulls. I love the feeling of my body coming alive, and as I look at the mirror behind the dumbbell rack, I try to see myself as Tanya described me. Maybe if I were the vain type I would flex, but to me it's just *me*, which at age forty is not bad at all. I am healthy, and I guess that outweighs everything else from an aesthetic point of view.

I shower before leaving the gym, anxiety building the whole way home. I try to call Marcus for some last minute advice or encouragement, but I can't reach him. Left alone with my nerves getting the best of me, I set the alarm on my cell phone and lie down to take a nap on the couch. Closing my eyes, I focus on my breaths, counting from one to ten several times before I feel myself drifting off.

When I awake, I can't remember my dream or the feeling of anxiety. I reach over and check my cell phone and realize that Tanya doesn't have my phone number. I walk over to my laptop and check for any instant messages, thinking to myself for the first time that we might need to find a more immediate way of contacting each other if things should evolve into more than late night chats.

As far as I know, I still have an hour before Tanya arrives, so I take another shower and put on the polo shirt and khakis that I ironed earlier this morning.

Glancing in the mirror, I think to myself, "I'm as ready as I'll ever be."

---

SEVEN O'CLOCK COMES AND GOES, while I sit on my couch, peeking through the blinds beneath the closed curtains. Occasionally I walk over to my computer and check for any messages before returning to the couch.

Eight o'clock comes and goes, and I begin to consider whether or not something bad has happened. I have no number to call, but I consider calling the Atlanta Police Department to check for any accidents. Another part of me whispers that I might have simply been stood up. Maybe this is just a game to her, getting a professor to step across that informal code of conduct to confess a romantic interest in her. I feel like such a sucker. Am I really that old creepy professor who gets off on young girls? I am suddenly flush with embarrassment and then fear. Could something like this come back to haunt me on my tenure review next year?

I stop cold. I'm overthinking this again, I know.

I turn off the lights in the den, and as my eyes adjust to the darkness, I walk into the kitchen and grab a banana. I peel it and take a bite. Through the blinds in the den I can see a pair of headlights pulling into my driveway. I walk closer to the window and immediately recognize Tanya's car. I see the headlights turn off and her door crack open so that the interior lights come on. It's definitely her.

She gets out of the car, and I can only make out that she is wearing a sleeveless light colored button-up shirt and a pair of khaki shorts. She walks toward the house, but her hands are empty.

---

I AM SO SURPRISED to see her that I open the door with the lights still turned off in the house.

"I'm sorry, Ed," she starts.

I don't really know what she's apologizing for, but I respond, "That's OK. What happened?"

Her face looks troubled, and instinctively I take her by the hand and usher her into the house. I reach over and turn on a lamp resting nearby.

"Have a seat," I say, pointing to the couch.

She walks over and sits down in the center of the couch, and I take a seat next to her.

"It's been a crazy day," she says, placing her hands on her knees and looking upward to gain some composure.

I nod attentively.

"Hey, let me start by apologizing for not getting a

chance to make dinner for you. It was in the plan, but plans change, you know."

I look at her curiously, not understanding what she is getting at. I wait for her to continue.

Finally, she says, "I broke up with Kevin today."

I don't know what that means for her or for me, but I know that break-ups are rarely pretty.

"Do you want to talk about it?" I ask.

She looks at me, and I can't make out what her expression means. It looks like a cross between pain and elation.

"I mean, I knew that sooner or later we would probably break it off, but I didn't wake up this morning thinking, you know, that this would be the day."

"Yeah."

"It's just that he—whoo," she starts, her voice going up an octave on the last word before she attempts to stabilize it, "that asshole just picked the wrong damn day, you know?"

"Yeah," I offer, trying not to get in the way of her thoughts.

"OK," she says, breathing deeply. "This is how it went down. He went to the pajama jam last night and we got into a fight on the way home."

"A fight? Like fists?"

"No, I mean an argument. I kept asking him about that girl over in Columbus, you know? Asking him if that baby was really his. He kept on saying 'no,' but then he got mad and said that it *was* his and that it was something that happened in his past and that I needed to just get past that. I was like 'hell no!' How do you get past a kid? He must think I got Boo Boo the Fool written across my forehead. So he kept calling me all this morning, and I let it go straight to voicemail. Finally, he shows up at my crib, and I'm getting ready to make your meal, and he starts getting all up in my face, saying stuff like I'm the one who's tripping. When I tell him that I don't want him anymore, he starts yelling on me. I told him that he can't yell at me—even if this wasn't my crib—but especially because it was, you know?"

She is talking quickly now, and I can tell that she's reliving the conversation as she recounts what happened, although I'm not quite understanding all that she's saying.

"Then he said that I could never find a man like him, so I needed to just accept facts and get over myself. And I was like 'what the—?', you know? Then I told him I was going out later anyway. He asked me with who, and I told him none of his business. I think that's when he saw all the food laid out. He was like, 'You cooking for this dude?' And I said 'Yes.' So then he flips the whole thing on me saying that I was the one who was cheating on him."

My stomach sinks, as I hear myself becoming a part of her story. This is definitely not what I wanted—getting pulled into a relationship gone sour. I wonder what I have gotten myself into.

"Did you tell him who you were cooking for?" I ask, trying to disguise the concern in my voice.

"No, but he thinks it's one of the frats from the party last night. I told him that I hadn't done anything with anyone, unlike his cheating ass. Then I started getting his stuff and throwing it at him. That's when he really got mad. I emptied out this drawer he had been using for when he stayed over. Gave him all of his shit back and told him to get the hell out of my house. And this fool acted like he didn't want to leave. He started throwing my food on the floor and stuff. It got real ugly. My roommate finally came home and threatened to call the cops on him. As soon as she picked up her cell phone to dial, he said, 'Fuck this' and left."

"Did he come back?" I ask.

"No. Just left, you know? And that's when it hit me that it was all over." She turns her face away from me. "I don't even know why I'm telling you all of this."

"It's OK. I want you to be able to talk to me."

"Yeah," she responds, brushing her hand across her eyes. Up till that point, I did not realize she was crying.

I place my hand on her back. "You want anything to drink?"

"No. I'm cool." She sits with her head downward, looking at her hands. "Hey, Ed, I'm sorry about your dinner. He messed up everything."

"Hey, I'm cool," I say, lifting what's left of my banana. "I was already eating when you got here."

She smiles and shakes her head. "You're crazy. You know that?"

"That's what they keep telling me."

I reach for the remote control on the coffee table. "Want to see what's on the TV?" I ask.

"Sure."

I fan through channels until she tells me to stop on *The Five Heartbeats*.

"I love this movie!" she says. "Can't nobody sang like ole Eddie King!" She says the word "king" so that it rhymes with "sang."

We laugh and settle back onto the couch.

"You want the lamp on?" I ask.

"No. I'm cool," she says.

I turn off the lamp, and before I know it, Tanya is snuggled against me on the couch, and I sense that the day is finally getting better for both of us.

# CHAPTER NINETEEN

I open my eyes, and it takes me a moment to realize that I am still lying on the couch. I look around for Tanya and immediately feel her head nestled against my chest, asleep. The TV is still on, and as my mind clears, I feel vaguely like I am in *Boomerang*, that Eddie Murphy movie with Halle Berry, where I am waking from a drowsy conversation about Star Trek. My arm is stiff, and I feel the urge to stretch, but I don't want to move her. I like the feeling of her lying on me.

I take my free hand and rub her arm softly. When I do this, she moans.

"I should probably get home," she mumbles. "What time is it?"

I continue rubbing her arm. "I don't know. I can't see a clock from here."

She sits up slowly, getting her bearings. Pulling her cell phone out of her purse, she says, "Damn. Kevin's been blowing me up."

I don't say anything.

"Yeah, I should probably leave and get home. It's almost two o'clock in the morning."

"You're welcome to spend the night. It's only a few hours," I offer.

She looks at me, and for a moment all I see is a woman fighting to stay awake. "I don't know, Ed," she says, blinking her eyes rapidly, as if to focus.

"It's been a long day. That's all I'm saying. I don't want you to fall asleep getting home. I don't think I could handle it if something happened to you."

She stands up slowly. "I'm just headed to Smyrna."

"Smyrna is farther than you think. Remember we're in Fairburn. That's at least half an hour or more. But I'll let you be the judge."

She stretches her arms and reaches for her purse. "Where is your bathroom?" she asks.

I point her down the hall and walk back into the den, taking a seat on the couch. I pick up the remote control, meaning to turn it off, when I accidently hit a few numbers that take me to a channel that plays music, jukebox-style. The music is mellow and soulful, but strangely seductive, as if someone, somewhere, is trying to set the mood. I look at a still photo of the album artwork and see Me'Shell Ndegeocello on the screen. The song drips sensuality and for a moment I find myself nodding to the rhythm, melting into her rich, full voice. The air around me starts to feel different, and I gradually become aware of how sexy I feel, the music insulating me from my nervousness.

"That's nice," Tanya says, stepping back into the den.

"It's sexy, isn't it?"

She looks at me, as if sizing me up. "Yeah. It's nice."

I look at the screen and see the song's title: "Outside Your Door." Looking at Tanya, I realize that I have no idea of how to read any of her mannerisms.

"Do we try this again?" I ask.

"Try what?"

"It just seems like every time we get together, our time is cut short."

"Yeah," she responds. "It does seem like that."

We stare at each other silently for a moment.

Finally, she opens her mouth. "A penny for your thoughts?"

I smile. "You don't want to know."

"What do you mean? Are they *that* bad?"

I don't say anything.

"How about this: if you could do any one thing right now, what would it be?"

I walk closer to her, closing the gap between us. She doesn't move.

Placing my hands tenderly on her cheeks, I lean in to kiss her. Before I reach her lips, she begins to speak.

"So this is what you want from me?"

I am so close to her that her breath tickles my nose. "I just want *you*," I whisper, placing my lips against her forehead. "I can't stop thinking about you."

I pull her into my embrace, kissing her neck softly. I feel her hands, interlocked against the small of my back. "I dream about you," I mutter between breaths, as I continue to kiss her. I feel the gentle stroke of her fingernails trail across the back of my head.

"You dream about me?" she says, her voice breathless and warm against my ear.

"Yes," I manage.

"And what do you dream about?" she says, holding my head close to the nape of her neck. The sweet smell of her skin reminds me of how good it feels to be so close to a woman.

"That I can touch you like this," I respond, moving my hands across her back, enjoying the warmth of her body beneath my fingertips.

She moans, and when I bring my face to hers again, she leans toward me and our lips touch.

I close my eyes and give in to everything bubbling beneath the surface.

———

SLOWLY MY MIND begins to come back into focus, and I realize that I am still holding her against the wall. She begins to lower her feet onto the floor, and I brace myself for the realization that there is nothing left for us to say. I am now just an anecdote. I am that professor that she had sex with that one time when she was in college.

"Penny for your thoughts?" she asks.

I start to speak, but close my mouth.

"That bad?"

I smile.

"I just wonder what happens now," I say.

"I don't know," she responds.

Her honesty doesn't hurt me like I thought it would.

She continues, "I don't normally do this."

"What? With someone older?"

"No. I'm not out there like that. I don't want you to think I'm all casual and loose. I only share myself with a guy if he's special."

"So I'm special?" I joke.

"You'd have to be," she says, smiling.

I cup her face with my hands and kiss her.

"So will I see you again?" I ask.

"Do you *want* to see me again?"

"Yes. Very much so."

"Well, then I guess we'll be seeing more of each other."

We walk over to the couch, where our clothes are scattered on the floor. She bends over and starts to get dressed. When she puts on her bra and begins buttoning her shirt, I ask, "Are you still leaving?"

She puts on a mock frown. "I don't want my roommate freaking out. Plus, we're supposed to be going to chapel in the morning on campus with our sorority sisters."

"Oh," I say. "Well, are you alert enough for the drive?"

"I'm good. Especially now." She grins at me coyly.

"OK," I say, smiling. "Well, can you call to let me know you make it home safely?"

"I can do that."

I call out my phone number as she punches it into her phone.

As much as it pains me to let her leave, I walk her out to her car. As she gets in and closes her door, I remind her to call me. She nods and smiles.

When I walk back into the house, I grab a comforter and lie down on the couch, where I can still smell traces of her in the fabric. Turning off the TV, I stare up at the ceiling, replaying everything that happened tonight. I lose track of time thinking about her, my erection still throbbing from the memory of her atop me.

Deep into my thoughts, my cell phone rings.

"Hello?"

"Ed, it's me. I'm home."

"Great," I say, suddenly feeling the weight of sleep knocking at the back of my eyelids.

"Make sure you save my number in your phone," she says.

"OK."

"Well, I'll talk to you later," she says. "Gotta get up early."

"You have sweet dreams, Tanya."

"You too, Ed."

## CHAPTER TWENTY

After I wake up early Sunday morning, I still have to remind myself that what happened earlier this morning had actually happened. She *was* here, and we were right here on this couch where I am lying now. I can barely make out slight traces of her scent, but the memories of her legs wrapped around me are still strong.

I walk into the kitchen and pour myself a glass of orange juice, my mind still adjusting to the weight of everything. I look at the couch and replay what I can remember. I remember carrying her across the room and pinning her against the wall. I put the glass down on the counter and walk over to it. My heart sinks as I realize that that was the place I had removed Charlotte's picture a week ago.

I stumble over to the couch and collapse facedown. I cannot even remember how I got into this situation. The last few weeks have been a blur, part of me feeling more alive than I have been in quite some time, the other part feeling as though I have betrayed the last fifteen years of my life.

WITH THE SILENCE of the house around me, it dawns on me just how reckless I have been. I don't even know her full name. There were just so many questions that I didn't even ask—for one reason or another—probably because I didn't want to disrupt the mood. How many assumptions did I make last night? I am stupefied by how careless I was. No protection. What in the world was I thinking?

She had just broken up with her boyfriend, and what did I do? I took advantage of her need to feel connected to someone. Or did I? I realize that I am incapable of knowing the exact subtext of what happened. I only know that I needed her last night, and it seemed like she needed me, too. That should be enough to steel my mind for now, but honestly, it doesn't.

I consider calling Marcus and getting his take, but I am not ready to go there. This is *my* secret, the one I alone share with Tanya, and I don't want to make that cheap by explicating the details to my brother with a play-by-play analysis. In fact, the only thing I want to do is talk to her about what happened.

When I finally glance at my phone, I see a text from Tanya that came through while I was sleeping. The message is short and simple: "Woke up feeling refreshed. Thank u 4 last nite. ;)."

I smile, hopeful, but still unsure.

# CHAPTER TWENTY-ONE

THE FIRST DAY OF SCHOOL IS ALWAYS INTERESTING. You have to set the pace for the semester with all of your students. I normally spend the first day of each class distributing the syllabus and discussing what's expected throughout the course. There's no real teaching on the first day. Still, that first class is where you establish your authority, or else your students will run over you for the rest of the semester.

My room is full of students who are looking to take my class as an easy elective. Survey of African-American Studies 201 is always like that. Teaching at a Historically Black College, I find that many of the students feel as if they are guaranteed no grade lower than a "B," simply because they played Martin Luther King, Jr. or Rosa Parks in their churches' black history programs. And teaching young people who feel like they already know everything is annoying and frustrating. That's one of the reasons I quiz often. There are not enough McDonald brochures on black history for students to shoot from the hip on my quizzes. Either you read the assignments or you learn to read them. I have little patience for people pontificating about what they don't know.

I do love teaching, though. I imagine that I fall into that cliché category of teachers who enjoy seeing the "light bulb" come on for that one student who struggled most of the semester. It's a wonderful feeling, almost like the high from a drug, and loving that high, most of us spend our careers chasing that feeling, hoping to experience it at least once a semester. Prior to that point, we all talk of giving up our teaching posts and going to work in the corporate world, getting paid what we're supposed to be worth.

Sure, we talk. That's part of our dialogue. But at the end of the day, we keep coming back.

---

BY LATE AFTERNOON, I can think of nothing but the sexy image of Tanya's body, in all of its glorious splendor. I remember the feel of her legs wrapping around my waist, her fingers easing up my back as she holds on to me. I can still feel her sliding up and down me, taking me in, making me feel as if I still exist—as if I still matter.

I look out the window of my office, gazing at the campus, its sprawling spaciousness populated by the faces of young black men and women. Maybe Tanya is somewhere down there.

As I gather my things to head home, I am unable to steel my thoughts. Even the wind kissing my face as I step out of the building reminds me of her lips. I am a mess, I know. I did not realize how much my body longed for companionship, and now I am beginning to worry that I'm making too big of a deal out of this situation. Maybe it was just sex after all—but to a person who has not been intimate in as long as I have, it feels like so much more.

Walking across campus to the faculty parking lot, I

see a group of students standing around in a circle. They must have just gathered, because I didn't see them earlier from my window. I can hear the chants and claps, and by the gawking of the freshmen, I can tell that one of the sororities is putting on an impromptu step performance.

I ease in closer, wondering if the female voices I hear chanting are those of Tanya's sorority. As I step up behind the group of spectators, I immediately realize that it is.

I search the sorors' faces, but their heads are down as they prepare to begin their next routine. One of them steps forward, her head still cast downward, but I know it's Tanya.

She lifts her head upward and begins chanting, "My sisters! I said, my sisters!"

"Yeah!" the others respond.

"Let's show them how the ladies of Zeta Delta Kappa set it off!"

Suddenly, Tanya lowers her head and sweeps her hands downward clapping very slowly. As she does her rhythm, the others wait patiently. When Tanya is finished and returns upright, the entire group goes into the same routine at nearly three times the speed she had just done it.

I find myself unable to look away. She looks sexy as she steps with the group. Her Greek lettered baby t-shirt fits snuggly against her body, complementing the denim shorts slowly riding up her thighs. I smile to myself.

The students around me jockey for better positions to watch the next chant, and I gradually step back. As much as I would love to stand around and continue watching Tanya, I realize that I'm the only faculty member there.

I suddenly feel old and out of place.

I take in one last glimpse of the step team, and I notice Tanya looking in my direction. Her lips peel into a slight smile. I know she can see me now. I nod my head slightly in acknowledgement and then turn to walk on to the faculty parking lot.

# CHAPTER TWENTY-TWO

"Well, maybe it just wasn't meant to be," my brother says. "You know there are always more fish in the sea. Or is that fishes, Mr. College Professor?" He laughs.

"Yeah, I guess you're right."

As I continue talking to Marcus while driving home, I wonder if I should have just told him the truth about Tanya, as opposed to lying about what happened. I find myself unable to believe everything that has happened so far, and now that I have officially crossed that line with her, I can't even bring myself to tell anyone about it—not even the one person who knows that I even like her.

"Little brother, I didn't see that one coming, I swear. From everything that you told me, it seems like she would have been on you like flies on shit. Break it down to me again how she backed out on you."

As I turn onto 85 South, I wonder how long I can keep up this façade. I am not the best liar, and with the questions Marcus continues to ask me, I wonder when I will put a chink in the armor of my story.

"She has a boyfriend she's pretty serious about," I say.

"I'm just not buying it. It doesn't make sense to me."

"Why not?"

"She's stepped out kind of far now. Both of you are out over a barrel. There's no reason for her to play that card now. You both stand to lose if this shit goes haywire."

"I'm not sure I buy that logic."

"That is," Marcus starts, "unless you're lying to me, little brother."

I can't tell if he's messing with me just to get a reaction, but it still makes me nervous. "Why would I lie to you?"

Right when I hear my voice, I know he has me. He was fishing around, and I played right into his hand.

"Oh shit, Ed! You hit it!"

"What? Man, please."

"Dude, it's too late to front now. You just tipped your hand."

As I listen to him, I realize that I will never understand how my brother can read me so well.

"You make it sound all bad," I say, looking to save face.

"Why didn't you just come right out with it? Lying to your own flesh and blood. CMB, baby! We all we got! We all we got!" he says, recalling one of his favorite lines from the movie *New Jack City*.

"Yeah," I say, trying to keep from smiling.

"It was good, too, wasn't it?" he says.

I am silent. I still can't believe my brother has me "kissing and telling."

"You don't have to say anything," he says. "I already know it was good. But you know what, little brother? It was good *for* you."

I wonder if he has a point. "I'm not saying anything else, Marcus."

"I feel you. Don't say anything then. Be all mysterious and cryptic with your shit, if that's the way you want to play it," he says, laughing. "I only have one question for you: when are you two hooking up again?"

"Now that's a good question," I respond. All I can say is, "Soon, I hope."

---

I PICK up some take-out on the way home when I realize that I have yet to grocery shop for anything meaningful to cook. If Kevin hadn't destroyed the food Tanya was preparing for me, I might have had something in the refrigerator I could heat up for dinner. As it stands, I am having Boston Market—again. I really should start back cooking, but I guess I'm clinging to the idea that the kitchen was where Charlotte would do her thing. She was always watching The Food Network looking for new dishes to prepare. She enjoyed cooking and often joked that she should go on the American version of *The Iron Chef* and challenge Bobby Flay or Cat Cora. I would smile at her and nod. She even started me cooking when she bought me a G. Garvin cookbook for Christmas one year. But all of that feels like a lifetime ago. I still haven't been able to muster the enthusiasm to cook anything myself since Charlotte passed.

As I poke at the rotisserie, I wonder what will happen next. I don't think I'm supposed to call her, but I'm not totally sure. I have the feeling she is the one who will control when we see each other again and that my role is to simply sit back and be there for her when she calls. That's a bit passive for my taste, but I'm so rusty at this that I can't even strategize the most basic of things. I haven't dated, or whatever you want to call this, in over seventeen years, and back then, things were very different. Things were intense, but they moved just a bit slower. I didn't even kiss Charlotte until our third date, and it was more than a month before we moved past second base. Dating these days, from what I hear, is much like using a computer with broadband, rather than the dial-up from those AOL discs I used to collect: people want what they want now, not later. I feel like I'm the slow guy in the right lane of the interstate and everyone is whooshing past me.

I finish part of my chicken and put the rest in the refrigerator for lunch tomorrow. I walk over to the couch and lie down, closing my eyes. I sniff the air, hoping that her perfume is still there, but it is gone. Other than my memory, there is no reminder of what happened, just an empty space on the wall where Charlotte's picture used to be.

A tinge of guilt rolls up in my stomach again, and I wonder if I am doing the right thing. I wish I could get a confirmation that I am not being a bad widower, that I am not disrespecting my wife's memory. I have heard of men remarrying a year after the passing of their wives, and I even heard about one widower who was introduced to his second wife by his first wife prior to her death. At first I found the idea odd, but now that I am here, I can understand it on some level. I am used to having someone around me. Who I am is set up around my having a life partner, and now that I am alone, I am a wreck. I don't know how to be by myself, and honestly, I don't want to be.

Part of me wants to believe that Charlotte would want me to be happy, but the other part doesn't really know what to make of it. Maybe I am just telling myself what I want to hear. Whatever the case, I need to decide what will be and how I will approach this new chapter. One thing is sure: I have reached the middle of the lake. Either I turn around or keep swimming.

# CHAPTER TWENTY-THREE

Tanya calls me shortly after ten o'clock and is pulling into the driveway around eleven. We don't make it past the foyer this time. Before I realize it, she is on top of me, pushing down on my chest so that my back is pinned to the carpet. It is only when she drops herself onto my chest from exhaustion that she even says "hello." I can't complain, though. I could learn to appreciate such a greeting.

She puts on her baby t-shirt and panties and heads for the couch. "How was your first day back?" she asks.

I wipe the sweat from my face and collect my clothes from the floor. "It was all right. Nothing major happened today, so those are always good days."

She smiles. "I saw you this afternoon."

"Yeah. I couldn't help but notice you. You look pretty sexy when you step."

"Thanks," she responds. "We're getting closer to rush, so it's important that people see us so they know that we're strong on the yard."

I put on my boxers and a t-shirt and sit down beside her. She immediately stretches her legs across my lap and smiles at me.

"I take it your week is off to a good start," I say, taking one of her feet in my hands and massaging it.

She closes her eyes, relaxing her head against one of the throw pillows. "Mmm hmm," she moans, her lips sealed in a smile. "That feels nice."

"Can I ask you something?"

"Sure."

"What is *this*?"

"What do you mean?"

"This. Here. What we're doing."

She chuckles softly. "Do we have to name it?"

I swallow. "No. I was just curious."

She lifts her leg from my lap. "I need to use your bathroom."

"Help yourself," I say, shifting so that she can stand.

When she walks away, I feel embarrassed for having asked the question. Being off the market for over seventeen years, I find that I don't know what to say in these situations anymore.

I pick up the remote control lying on the coffee table and turn on the flat screen. I scan channels for the hell of it—just to have something to do. I'm trying to ease my mind and not get too ahead of myself, but I can't help but wonder how long all of this will last.

"Ed," I hear Tanya call from down the hall.

"Yes?"

"Can you come here?"

"Sure," I say, hopping up from the couch. I walk toward the bathroom, and when I don't see her, I call out, "Where are you?"

"Back here. In the bedroom."

My heart catches in my chest, and for a moment I can't breathe. I can already envision the framed photographs of Charlotte on the nightstand next to my bed, the wedding photos on the wall. I can even remember the hospital bed we had put in our bedroom, which sat perpendicular to the bed that had been ours.

Now Tanya is standing in this room, this sacred space, and I don't what to think—or feel.

As I enter the room, Tanya reads my expression.

"I'm sorry," she says, putting a framed photograph of Charlotte back on the nightstand.

I don't know if she is saying that she is sorry for walking back into this room or if she is sorry for my loss. I swallow hard and try to relax my creased brow.

"She was very beautiful," Tanya says, stepping away from the nightstand.

I walk past her and pick up the photograph she has just put down. I look at it, as if seeing it for the first time. Charlotte is wearing a heavy leather jacket as she stands in front of Stone Mountain. It's one of the last outings we had before she got sick. I remember the day all too clearly, how we went out to eat dinner in downtown Atlanta after leaving the park and came back here, where we made love for the rest of the evening. Until Tanya came in here, the picture had not been moved, except for dusting, in nearly two years.

I put the photograph back in its place and turn to face Tanya. She stares at me, not knowing what to say.

"Why did you come in here?" My voice is firm, and I feel as though I am about to lecture a child.

"I don't know," she starts. "I was just walking down the hall, and I saw a picture of this beautiful woman." I see the fear building in her eyes, as she realizes she has done something wrong. "I just wanted to tell you something."

"Yeah. What?"

"Maybe I should tell you later. You don't look very happy."

I exhale slowly. I look at her, then look away. "What do you want me to say?"

"Say something, 'cause right now I'm feeling like you don't want me here."

I tense my jaw, and it's as if every photograph of

my wife starts glowing across the room like Christmas lights. Then the guilt pangs kick me in my gut.

"I should leave," Tanya says, turning and walking back toward the den.

I want to follow her, but I can't bring myself to move—or even open my mouth. I feel as though Charlotte is watching me, waiting to see what I will do. I stand still, paralyzed by my thoughts.

I hear the door close at the other end of the house, and I know that Tanya is gone.

As I turn to look back at the photograph on the nightstand, I realize that Charlotte is gone, too.

# CHAPTER TWENTY-FOUR

MY 10 O'CLOCK CLASS HUDDLES IN GROUPS, working on a project I have assigned them. Eyes float above opened laptops, and I know that some of them are doing the work—those who are serious about learning—and others are checking their social media accounts or checking e-mail. Normally I would walk around proctoring their activities, but today I don't feel like doing much of anything.

I had momentarily considered calling in sick this morning so I could lie in bed and host a one-man pity party, but I'm too old to be acting like that. So I go through the motions, maintaining the status quo.

Soon the class ends and the students drop their assignments on my desk, before heading out. I stuff the papers into my leather satchel and walk back to my office. I'm tired, not physically, but emotionally. Last night I tried again to dream of Charlotte, and when that didn't happen, I found myself thinking about Tanya. I really messed that up. I didn't even call her last night to check on her. I'd been a complete ass, not all that different than that Kevin guy she had just been dating. I want to pick up my cell phone and call her, but I know she's probably in class, and even if she weren't, she probably wouldn't want to talk to me. I just didn't know how to react when I saw her with Charlotte's photograph.

Now as I sit looking out of my office window, I hope I will see her walking by. Maybe she'll look up and see me in one of the windows and smile, letting me know that everything is all right. But I can't make out one student from the next, and with the sunrays slanting against the building, my face would be hidden by its reflection from anyone who cared to look upward.

---

DR. CORDELL MURPHY is full of far more shit than I thought he was. I thumb through his journal article for the third time, citing inconsistencies and other problems. Part of me just wants to walk into his office and tell him what a fool he is for showing up to a battle of wits completely unarmed, but I remind myself that he's actually doing me a favor. I can get several more articles published by just going back and forth with this fool, and at this point everything works for the greater good of tenure.

As I make notes on my response, I shudder at the thought I have to sit on a committee with him. What was once a scholarly article has now become the makings of a war among colleagues, and while I plan to win this particular war, I hate the fact that my antagonism is reserved from another Ellison-Wright faculty member, especially one with whom I have to work.

When my office hours are finished, I walk across the campus to the faculty parking lot. I scan the yard for Tanya, but I don't see her.

As I put my bag on the floorboard of the passenger's side of the car, I pick up my cell phone and dial my brother. He picks up on the second ring.

"Ed-brunski," Marcus greets me, picking from one of his many nicknames for me.

"How's it going?" I respond.

"Moving like a laxative, my brother, like a laxative."

I chuckle, as I steer out of the parking lot and off campus.

"So what are you up to?" he asks.

I tell him all about last night, and wait quietly while he digests it.

"Mmm hmmph," he finally grunts.

"So what should I do?"

He inhales deeply and says, "You gotta answer that one yourself. Clearly, you might not be ready to push on, but I kind of think that deep down you are. You just won't give yourself permission to go there."

I nod. Then I realize that he can't see me. "I feel you," I finally say.

"Let me ask you a question. Do you like this Tanya girl?"

"Yes."

"And is she worth the effort you're putting into this?"

"Yes."

"Well, then you might want to just go with it," Marcus says.

I ponder his words for a moment before asking, "How do I fix what happened last night? She probably thinks I'm crazy or something."

"Ed, everyone makes mistakes. If she likes you, she just might for forgive you for this one. You won't know until you talk to her."

"So I should call her or wait for her to call me?"

He chuckles. "If you're waiting for her to call you, then you might be waiting a long time. In theory you're the one who fucked up, so *you* need to clear the air."

I consider this, before saying, "Thank you."

"No problem. Just do me one favor."

"What's that?"

"Cut yourself some slack and try to get back to en-joying life."

I nod, thanking him, before hanging up and ex-iting onto Interstate 85 South.

---

*No. 31*

> *I don't know why your kisses scare*
> *Me, like trolls lurking beneath old bridges*
> *Or ghosts that swing from the nooks*
> *Of huge Dixie oaks. You hold me*
> *Like Nina, your spell, wicked with desire,*
> *Drawing me from my cocoon to be*
> *Born within the beauty of your lips.*

---

ONCE I GET HOME, I call Tanya. When her voicemail comes on, I fumble to find the words to leave as a message.

"This is Ed. I just wanted to talk with you about last night—apologize to you. Uh, you can call me back or I can call you or, well, you know. I just hope that we can talk some time tonight. I'll be online, too."

By now I sound like a bumbling fool, so I offer a quick closing. "Take care, and I hope to hear from you soon." I hang up the phone to spare myself further em-barrassment.

Less than a minute later my phone rings. I glance at the caller ID and smile when I see Tanya's name.

"Hey," I answer. "I was hoping you would call me back."

"Who the fuck is this?" The voice is deep and much harsher than I expected.

I look at the cell phone display, and it clearly says "Tanya" on it.

"Hello?" I say again.

"Bitch, I just asked you who the fuck this is," the guy says again.

I don't say anything.

"Don't call back, or I'll fuck you up, Eadie, or who ever the fuck this is."

The phone clicks, and I stand there looking at it. My mind is a jumble, but it slowly dawns on me that Kevin must have gotten hold of Tanya's cell phone. Still shaking off the phone threat, I replay the name that he called me. Eadie?

"Eadie," I say over and over until I hear the letters that make up my nickname. Rather than put "Ed" into her phone, she went with a feminine name so no one would notice if they used her phone, I'm guessing.

Everything might have worked out well, too, if I hadn't just called.

I am too shocked to even be angry about that boy cursing me out. Still a part of me wonders what I have gotten myself into. I need to talk to her now more than ever.

In an effort to collect myself, I lie down on the couch. When I awake, it's nearly midnight, our usual talk time.

I rush to log on to WEB instant messenger, hoping to find her online. And although I wait around for an hour, she never comes on. I look at my cell phone, willing it to ring, and when it doesn't, I close my laptop and head to bed.

# CHAPTER TWENTY-FIVE

WITH ALL OF THE TOOLS AVAILABLE FOR communicating with someone, I am flustered at how I've managed to be locked out of Tanya's world. With the cell phone not an option and our inability to connect over WEB instant messenger, I can only hope to run into her physically. At one point, I actually consider sending her an e-mail through her school account, but I realize I don't even know her last name. It's probably for the better that she doesn't know I am trying so hard to connect with her. I wouldn't want her thinking that I was crowding her.

I try to get into a daily routine that does not include her, but I find my thoughts drifting back to her, my mind stuck in daydreams of the two times we made love. Is that what I'd call it though? Did we make love? I'm skeptical to think of it all as just *fucking*, but maybe that's what it was. And maybe that phase is over and she's onto someone else. She doesn't strike me as that kind of person, but then again, I realize I don't really know all that much about her.

The irony is that the department secretary, Missy Alexander, has taken to leaving little Post-Its on my desk at work, words of encouragement and the occasional Bible verse, almost as if she can sense the heavy level of sinning I'm involved in. I thank her and try not to read any more deeply into the timing of her actions. After all, I am the king of assumptions.

By the beginning of the weekend, I have all but resigned myself to the fact that Tanya is no longer interested in me. I still log on to WEB instant messenger on Friday night, hoping to see her so I can at least bring some closure to the situation.

When I see her logged on, my stomach is immediately filled with butterflies. I type, "hi" and push send.

Then I wait.

She responds within seconds, and for that, I am truly relieved.

"What's up?"

"I'm sorry," I type. No point in beating around the bush.

"For what?"

"Last week—with the picture."

"Oh. OK."

A minute passes before either of us types anything else.

"I tried to call you," I type.

"I know. Kevin stole my phone."

"Did I get you in trouble?"

"Not really. It's over with him."

"Do you have your phone now?"

"Yes."

"Can you call me?" I type.

"Hold on."

A few seconds later my cell phone rings. I grab it quickly and place it to my ear. "Hello?"

"Hey, you," she says, her voice warm and soft. It's as if we never missed a day of talking. I want to reach through the phone and hold her.

"I'm so sorry about before," I say again. "I didn't know what to think when I saw you in my bedroom. I just overreacted."

"I understand," she said. "I shouldn't have been in there anyway. It's not like you invited me in there."

"Still, I was tripping."

"I'll forgive you, if you forgive me."

"Done," I say, relieved.

She chuckles lightly, and for the first time all week I feel that familiar rhythm of talking to her.

"What happened this week? I didn't think I would ever hear from you again."

She is quiet for a moment before answering. "After falling out with Kevin again, I decided to take some 'me' time."

I want to ask her about Kevin, but decide to keep the focus on us instead. "How are you feeling?"

"I'm better."

"Tanya?"

"Yes."

"I want to see you," I blurt out.

"When?"

"Now."

I hear her breathing, but she does not speak.

I wait patiently.

"You asked me about what it was that we're doing here," she starts. "I'm just getting out of a relationship, so I'm not looking for anything serious. And I know you probably aren't ready for anything serious either."

I want to ask her why she thinks I don't want anything serious, but I shut out those thoughts and listen.

"I don't know what we're doing," she says. "I just know I like being around you."

"I like being around you, too. That's why I want to see you."

"It's almost midnight, though."

"I know. I want you to stay the night."

"Are you sure about that?"

I take a deep breath. "Yes. Or I could go over there."

She laughs. "Yeah, right. My roommate would never let me live that one down."

I laugh along.

"So you're coming?" I ask.

Although I sense reluctance in her voice, I am relieved when she finally answers, "Yes."

---

I HAVE REMOVED all of the pictures from the walls and even those on the nightstand by the time Tanya arrives. I know I will put a few of them back up in various places in the house, but for now, I put them in the closet on one of the shelves.

When Tanya pulls into the driveway and gets out with a backpack, it dawns on me that we are well past the point of mere curiosity. She has a pretty good idea of how I will touch her, and she knows that when she leaves I will want her even more. Our bodies are no longer strangers, and if we both consent, neither will our minds.

We embrace when she walks into the house, and I hope she feels the desire rolling off my skin in waves.

"I've missed you," I say, my cheek against hers.

"I've missed you, too," she responds.

I move to kiss her, and she allows me. It feels different from the other times, though. There's a *knowing* in the way we touch each other, and it seems as though something other than lust is carrying us back to my bedroom.

I undress her by the bed. She lies down, and I proceed to kiss her from her forehead down to her toes. As I work my way back up her legs, I lift them over each of my shoulders and bury my tongue inside of her. She rocks her hips against my face, her hands gripping my head tightly.

Our movements evolve as we find ourselves intertwined in ways that can only be felt, not planned. When I enter her, my thrusts are deep, and I hold her tightly, her legs hugging my back, as we move fluidly with each other. Her gasps dance against my lips, and as we build to a climax, we disappear into each other.

Afterwards we lie across the sweat-soaked bed, her head nuzzled in the crook of my arm. She does not comment on the absence of the photographs. She only exhales sweetly against my chest.

I close my eyes and try not to think of anything, just enjoying the feel of her fingertips swirling in small circles across my shoulder.

———

"Can I ask you a silly question?" I say, as she rises from my bed and begins to dress the following morning.

"OK."

"What is your last name?"

She laughs, buttoning her shirt. "Hendrix."

"Like Jimi?"

"Yeah."

"So it's Tanya Hendrix?"

She laughs again, shaking her head. "Actually Tanya's my middle name."

I sit up, my back propped against the headboard. "So what's your first name then?"

She pulls up her jeans and fastens them, her blushing face looking downward. She seems to be playing with the idea of whether or not she will tell me. I stare at her, smiling, in hopes she will not feel so embarrassed.

"Oreetha," she says, shaking her head as if she were the victim of a drive-by naming.

"Aretha?" I say.

"No. With an O and two Es."

"Good lord," I mutter before I realize that I am making the comment aloud.

"I know," she says. "That's my grandmother's name."

I nod, understanding her preference for her middle name. As I rise from the bed, I realize that her name feels really familiar, but I can't place it. Maybe I'm just in an Aretha Franklin mood or something.

"I know that neither of us is looking for anything serious, but I was wondering if you were seeing anyone else," I say.

She sits down on the bed and watches me dress. "I don't have time for any of that. Not with school and my sorority. I can't even work this semester like I had planned. So the short answer to your question is that *you're* the only guy I'm kicking it with."

"So that makes this situation pretty exclusive, right?"

She ponders this. "Exclusive like I'm only having sex with you? If that's what you mean, then yes."

What she says feels safe, not obligatory. We are just two people finding comfort in each other's company. And maybe that's all we really need to be.

When she leaves later in the morning, I watch her from just inside the threshold of my front door. I would prefer my neighbors not speculate about my personal life, so I avoid walking her out to her car.

Once Tanya drives out of view, I consider returning to the bedroom and lying down to relive the previous evening. I walk over to the couch instead. I lay my head against a throw pillow and inhale. There is no scent there, no memory. There is only me.

I fall asleep, and this time I am dreamless.

## CHAPTER TWENTY-SIX

CHARLOTTE AND I GOT MARRIED IN THE GAZEBO of a small park just outside of Memphis. The ceremony lasted only twenty minutes, which served me well, since I was so nervous anyway. Marcus would occasionally lean over from his post as my best man and tell me not to lock my knees. "It's too hot out here, little brother. You could pass out." In fact, with my mind completely blank, I could only hold on to two thoughts throughout the ceremony: not locking my knees and responding "I do" to every question put to me by the minister. The only time I really snapped out of my daze was when I kissed Charlotte. At that point I felt that we were alone in the shade of some giant magnolia tree, sharing a private moment. When I opened my eyes, I could hear people fawning and clapping.

I can still remember carrying her across the threshold of the small apartment we were renting. Back then, everything seemed possible. We were two kids in love, and the world lay before us like a yellow brick road.

That first apartment was so small that we didn't have enough space to put all of our things in it. I decided to put most of my stuff in storage so she wouldn't have to throw out any of her things. Our kitchen didn't leave much space either. The thin space between the stove and the sink didn't allow either of us to stand back-to-back, although neither one of us was very large. The worst part, though, was the toilet, which made a violent five-minute groan after being flushed. Even worse, the flushing strength was so weak that we had to make a habit of flushing twice. Fewer things could help a person to realize the reality of marriage quicker than walking into a bathroom and seeing remnants of your spouse's fecal sediment sitting at the bottom of the toilet bowl.

That first year was tough, but we kept up with our bills through student loans and academic fellowships. When I finally got my first teaching job, we went out to celebrate at a Chinese food buffet, one of the few places we went to when we were in a position to splurge. In those days, as cliché as it might sound, all we had was each other—which suited me just fine, but made her family dislike me all the more.

On one of their visits to our apartment, Charlotte's father pulled me aside and point-blank asked me, "So is it your intention to make my daughter live the rest of her life in section 8 housing?"

"No, sir," I responded. I knew our digs were not great, but I didn't think that they were as bad as he was inferring they were. I gritted my teeth and tried to steady my expression. "Things are starting to go well for us, and we should be moving out at the end of the lease."

"When I met you, I wondered if you'd be able to take care of my daughter. Now that you're married, I'm still wondering the same thing."

I realized right then and there that he and I would never have a good relationship with each other. If he didn't have the basic faith I could provide for his daughter, then he was no friend of mine. Sadly, it seemed whatever Charlotte's father thought of me, it became the family's view as well. I thought all of that madness would have ended when Charlotte and I moved to Mississippi and then on to Georgia, but it didn't.

"Why do your parents hate me so much?"

"They don't hate you," Charlotte responded. "They just have their own views about the kind of life they expect me to have."

"Well, I might not have the ability to give you everything that they can give you, but I can give you everything I have," I said.

"Baby, you don't have to prove a thing to me. I know you love me, and that's all that matters. You're a good husband."

"What about your family?"

"Baby, the only family you need to be worried about is this one," she said waiving her index finger between the two of us.

From then forward, I swore not to let her family get to me. We had even succeeded at getting along during Charlotte's illness, but now that she was gone, they had disappeared. I have not heard anything from any of them since the funeral. I guess now that the link between us is no longer there, they have no obligation to keep me as a part of their lives.

It's probably for the better that I never grew to count on them for anything anyway.

---

IN THOSE HOLLYWOOD MOVIES, the widower is usually wracked with so much heartbreak that he spends the next few years of his life suicidal, longing to be with his wife again. I remember once watching a movie where Robin Williams went inside of one of his deceased wife's paintings to find her, ultimately searching for her in the depths of Hell. If novelists and filmmakers had their way, I would be tossing stones into a lake out in the middle of the woods, talking with my wife's ghost. And I'm not even saying that a widower's grief does not run so deep that it can be paralyzing, but there's a difference between living with pain and being a character in a movie based on a Nicholas Sparks novel.

Watching Charlotte wither away was the most painful thing I have ever experienced. When she left me, I just wanted to crawl up inside of myself and stay there, buried in the dark emptiness of my heart. I don't know what would have happened if my brother didn't step in and pull me back from the ledge. Now I want to live again. I love the feeling of the autumn sun pushing through the grayness of a cool day. I smile when I hear Minnie Riperton's voice on the radio station. I am trying to find those good memories to cherish, but if I were to sit still, maybe—just maybe—the darkness would sweep over me again. And I don't want to go there.

Tanya has kept my mind away from the darkness. We have been doing this unnamed thing that we do for over a month. She spends at least three days a week at my house, usually on the nights after she finishes the pledging activities of her sorority. She arrives late, and as soon as I let her in, we head back to the bedroom. When we are lying naked, holding each other, she tells me about her day, and I tell her about mine. We are not a couple, yet we are. We don't love each other, yet we are lovers. At least that's what I keep telling myself.

# CHAPTER TWENTY-SEVEN

"LET'S GO AWAY FOR THE WEEKEND," TANYA SAYS, scrambling eggs on an early Saturday morning.

I am sitting at the table in the dining room area, just outside of the kitchen, with a copy of *Ebony* lying open in front of me. "Sure. Did you have any place in mind?"

"Not really. It's just that I know we can't really go out around here without stirring up a shit storm, so I figured we could drive somewhere people didn't know us and actually do things that couples do. Don't get me wrong. I love coming over here, but I sometimes feel like a vampire hiding from the sunlight. Know what I mean?"

"OK. So let's go somewhere today."

"Really? Are you serious?"

I smile. "Well, you already have a bag packed. I can put together one and we can hit the road."

"I would really like that," Tanya responds.

"Now we just have to figure out if we want to drive into Alabama, two hours away; South Carolina, two and a half hours away; or stay in state and drive toward Columbus or Savannah, which would take between two and five hours, depending on which one we pick."

"Let's get out of Georgia, *please*."

After breakfast, we load up my car and head toward Birmingham, Interstate 20 West blazing brightly ahead of us.

---

WE GET a suite at the Hampton Inn in Hoover, next to the Riverside Galleria just outside of Birmingham. We are close enough to nice restaurants and shopping, while still being able to see the gorgeous low Alabama mountains from our window.

Tanya insists that a walk through the Galleria will be a good way for us to stretch our legs. When we enter the spacious mall, I suddenly become self-conscious. I feel like I look every bit of my age and that I will receive sneers from the people we pass. "Look at that fine ass woman with the old ass dude." My stomach tightens another notch when Tanya reaches for my hand, interlocking her fingers with my own. She senses my tension and stops in her tracks.

"What's wrong? We're not in Atlanta. No one knows us here," she says. The look on her face makes it abundantly clear that she really wants this trip to work out well. She has been so patient with me up till now that I feel I owe her to help this trip be what she wants it to be.

"I'm just tripping. Feeling like an old man and all, but maybe it's just in my head."

She chuckles. "Here I am thinking that women will think I don't deserve to be with a brother as fine as you, and here *you* are, doing the same damn thing."

I know she's just flattering me, so I soften up a bit.

"Kiss me," she says.

"Here?"

"Just do it. Don't think about it."

I lean in slowly to kiss her, and she quickly grabs the

sides of my face pulling me closer to her, where she kisses me deeply, her tongue taking control of my mouth. She punctuates the kiss by reaching around and squeezing my behind with one of her hands. When she finishes, she pats my behind, loops her arm around mine, and says to me in an assertive, yet sexy, tone, "This weekend you are my man, so I need you to act like you're the man who rocks my world every time he touches me. OK?"

I nod and smile. "Let's do this."

From that point, each step we take is taken with the confidence that what we are doing is not taboo. We are leading with our hearts and not our heads, and I must confess it is a beautiful thing.

AFTER A SURF and turf dinner at one of the gourmet restaurants down the street from the hotel, we find ourselves nestled in the back of a bookstore, seated on a bench with her legs perched on my lap, as I read Pablo Neruda love poems to her. She listens to the translated words of the Chilean poet, her eyes closed, a smile on her face. As I read, I glance at her occasionally, watching her absorb each word. I wonder if I will ever let her read any of the poems I have been writing or if I should keep those thoughts to myself. There is just as much of Tanya in those words as there is Charlotte.

"Ed," she says, interrupting me. "Let's go back to the room. Now."

I start to close the book. "You sure you don't want to hear the rest of this poem first?" I joke.

"No. I want you to take me back to the hotel and fuck me until I can't remember my name—that is if you don't mind."

Her smile brings me to my feet, my fingers interlocking with hers, as we make haste toward the store's exit.

---

No. 39

*She pushes the ceiling away from us,*
*Leaving exposed our small bodies, far from*
*The closest star. We are the only*
*Matter that matters, this ball of energy,*
*Words and breath and skin and lust,*
*Wrapped like woven threads, an onyx cocoon,*
*Hoping to one day fly far away.*

---

"ARE YOU STILL AWAKE?" she asks in the early hours of the morning. We are draped across each other, naked, a disheveled bed sheet pushed down near our legs. Outside of our window is the soft glow of city lights against a deep blackness.

"Yes," I say, leaning over and kissing her.

"Something's been on my mind a lot lately, and I just wanted to know what you thought about it."

"Go ahead," I say, rubbing her arm softly with my thumb.

"I know we said that we weren't going to get serious or anything, but it's starting to feel like that's what we're doing." She pauses and sits up. She turns on the lamp next to the bed and faces me. "How do you feel about me? I mean, for real."

As I adjust myself in the bed, I realize that this conversation has been in the making for a while. I'd been asking myself the exact same question over these past several weeks, afraid to commit to an answer that would be ultimately unrequited. Yet, here is Tanya bringing up this very concern. "I have very strong feelings for you."

"Does that mean that you love me?"

I smile, unsure of where this is headed. "Why are we having this conversation? Didn't you say that you wanted to keep this as uncomplicated as possible?"

"I know, but there are so many things I want to tell you, and I don't know if I can say them to you unless I know how you really feel about me."

Her words are confusing, and I don't know whether she wants me to profess my love for her first so she can do the same or if there is something else she is hinting at. Instead of answering her question, I counter back with one of my own. "Do you love *me*?"

"Yes," she says matter-of-factly. There is no hesitation in her voice. It's as if she has known this fact for quite some time and has chosen to arbitrarily withhold it until it served a greater purpose. "I love you, even though I know that it's probably dangerous for me to feel this way. Still, you haven't answered my question. Do you love me, too?"

I look into her eyes and a memory of Charlotte singing on stage the night we met crosses my mind. The memory blends almost seamlessly with Tanya's face from that first night at Jean-Louis's. I hear the sweet song of Charlotte's voice and see the tender, agile movements of Tanya's body, its fluid dance speaking to the beauty of the space around her. I know I should feel divided, but I feel strangely enmeshed in a warm glow, as if what I am feeling is natural and real. I take Tanya's hand in mine and say, "Yes, I love you."

I don't know what these words mean to either of us in the context of our relationship, as we are still hiding from public eyes.

"I'm glad you said that," she responds. "Or better yet *relieved*. No one wants to be the only one in that boat."

I nod. "True."

"I know we've been talking around a lot of things since we started spending time together, and I'm tired of doing that. I want to be able to tell you what I'm really thinking and know that you love me enough to not judge me."

"I understand. What's on your mind?"

Tanya takes a deep breath before she begins. "You asked me about my father a while back, and I told you I didn't deal with him. I just wanted to tell you why."

My stomach tightens anxiously as I fight not to let my imagination get ahead of her.

"I led you to believe that it was just my mom and me and that I didn't have any other brothers or sisters. That's not true. I have a half-sister. She's four-years-old." She pauses again. "See, when I was in high school, my father became involved with my best friend, Carrie. I didn't know it was going on, but when she got pregnant, she confessed to me that it was my dad's. Needless to say, that situation destroyed our home. My parents got divorced, Carrie had the baby, and my father ended up moving out to Seattle, leaving all of us behind."

I don't know what to say to her as I listen to her explain how she hasn't seen him in years and has never met her half-sister, as she and Carrie don't talk anymore. She goes on to explain that her mother has started dating a guy, who, in Tanya's opinion, is far too young for her. I want to remind Tanya that I am a little over twice her age, but I don't. There are clearly a lot of unresolved issues throughout her entire family, everyone desiring to be with someone whose age is so far from his or her own that it begs the question of whether there is any psychological damage resulting from the father's initial transgression. And now I am willingly enmeshed in this curious situation.

"Do you think you are attracted to me because, in

a way, you want to get revenge for what your father did to you and your mother?" I ask.

"No. I really care about you. I think it's all coincidental."

"It's a big coincidence."

"I know what you're thinking now. You're thinking that I'm seeking a father figure and that I'm subconsciously trying to be closer to my father by being close to you," she says. "I've thought about us a lot, and I just don't believe that has anything to do with it. I have known for a while that I loved you, but I waited until tonight to tell you because I wanted to be sure that I wasn't trying to make this something that it wasn't."

"Then why are you telling me all of this now?"

"So you'll never have to wonder," she responds, then adds, "and it gives you the freedom to tell me that you're not with just because I remind you of your late wife."

This time it is I who takes the deep breath. "I can't say that you have never reminded me of her, but I can honestly say that I have come to love you in a way I never thought possible since Charlotte passed away. It hasn't even been a year, so I can't say that she's completely out of my system, or will ever really be, but I can say that my time with you has opened up doors in my heart that I thought were sealed shut. I don't know if that's what you want me to say or not, but I know it's true. And it's true that I love you and that I'm here for you."

She nods her head knowingly, as if my words don't surprise her. "So here we are," she finally says, "two broken people trying to mend each other."

She laughs and I laugh along, although we both know there is nothing funny about her words.

"So what do we do now?" she asks.

"What do you mean?"

"Do we continue our midnight escapades or so we move this relationship into the daylight?"

"I want to," I start, "but I have to be careful. *We* have to be careful, at least until you graduate."

Tanya nods. "Yeah. I keep forgetting about the professor/student thing."

"Yeah. And I'm up for tenure next year. I'm not sure this situation would go over well with the committee."

"Why is tenure so important to you?" she asks.

"For fifteen years I dragged Charlotte all over the South, from school to school, and the goal of it all was to get tenure somewhere. Ellison-Wright is the only school that has offered me this opportunity for security. If I get tenure here, I will have a job until I retire, and that was what Charlotte and I had been working on. It feels like, by finishing the process, I won't have wasted all those years of her life, all those sacrifices that we had to make."

"I see," Tanya responds. She is quiet for a moment. "I guess you're right," she finally says. "I guess I should be careful, too, since I'm on scholarship."

That's when it hits me. Oreetha Hendrix is one of the recipients of a presidential scholarship overseen by my committee.

"I don't know why I didn't put this together sooner," I say, floored by the extra level of inappropriateness that has been added to our relationship.

"What? My scholarship?"

"I was actually assigned to the Presidential Scholarship Committee after I returned from my sabbatical. We are the ones who renew your scholarship each semester. I swear I didn't know. Since I met you, you have always been Tanya to me. It never crossed my mind that the committee would know you by a different name."

Tanya chuckles uncomfortably. "Well, things continue to get more interesting, don't they?"

I reach out and pull her face closer to mine. We kiss, and the sun rises slowly behind us, shedding the first light on what we have become.

# CHAPTER TWENTY-EIGHT

SHORTLY AFTER CHARLOTTE AND I MOVED TO Fairburn, we made a drive to Savannah to tour the city. Charlotte had recently re-read John Berendt's book *Midnight in the Garden of Good and Evil* and insisted that we go and see the place in person, since it was only a few hours drive away. I thought we were going to see the architecture of the antebellum houses and maybe checkout Savannah State University's campus. It turned out that Charlotte's primary interest was to go to a cemetery to see a statue of a little girl holding bowls. She referred to it as the "bird girl" and after staring at the image of the statue, framed in Spanish moss, on the book cover, she insisted we go there.

"But that's a cemetery," I offered to little avail. "Someone is probably buried beneath that statue."

"I just want to see it up close."

When we got to the cemetery and circled around it several times, I became convinced that the statue wasn't even there anymore.

It didn't take long for us to realize the statue had been moved to the Telfair Museum of Art in Savannah because the family had tired of people casually socializing on their family plot. In the end Charlotte got to see her statue, but the macabre setting she had anticipated was severely muted by seeing it in its new environment.

The following morning, on the way back to Fairburn, I asked her, "What was it about that statue that made you want to see it?"

"I don't know," she said. "When I first saw the book cover, I didn't think the girl was holding bird feeders. To me, it seemed like she was holding scales and that she was actually being tilted toward one side. I just always imagined if those scales were representative of good and evil, then which one was she leaning toward? I just thought seeing her up close might help me to know."

The trip, rather than being romantic, felt more bizarre after her explanation. To her there was a beauty to the Southern Gothic, whereas I saw a graveyard and, later, a weird sculpture of a skinny white girl.

Even though that trip was several years ago, I still remember it as if it happened last week.

On Monday, after watching Clint Eastwood's film adaptation of *Midnight in the Garden of Good and Evil* with her roommate, Tanya mentioned to me that she would like to take a trip to Savannah for the weekend in lieu of sticking around town for the homecoming football game and various school events. When she mentioned her suggestion, a chill ran down my spine. How could it be possible that both Charlotte and Tanya were drawn to the same place for the same reason? It was definitely possible given the popularity of the book and film, but it felt like an eerie coincidence, nonetheless.

I am not looking forward to returning to Savannah, but I feel as though I owe Tanya for being so patient with me and the extreme level of privacy we are forced to cloak ourselves in here. And besides, we can't just keep going back and forth to Birmingham. To keep relationships fresh, you have to sometimes step outside of your comfort zone.

So if she wants to go see the "bird girl," then I guess we are going to see the bird girl.

---

"I AM SO SORRY," Tanya says when she arrives with her overnight bag. "My period is coming on, so we won't be able to do anything this weekend."

"That's all right. We don't have to have sex every time we see each other. We can just chill. How are you feeling?"

"I've been cramping a little." She puts down her bag near the couch in the den. "In fact, I need to go to the bathroom."

"Sure," I say, not really knowing what else to say. "Maybe we can send out for dinner. I'll dig up some menus online and we can talk about it when you come out."

"OK," she responds, grimacing slightly.

As she walks away, I open my laptop and start sorting through Yelp, looking for some positive reviews of restaurants nearby, preferably ones that deliver. While I comb through reviews, I wonder if Tanya will still feel up for going to Savannah tomorrow morning. Even though I would love to spend time with her away from Atlanta, I wouldn't be heart-broken if we didn't go there. I just don't want my memories of being there with Charlotte to interfere with forming new memories with Tanya.

"Ed," Tanya yells from down the hall. "Come here. Please!"

I run to the bathroom in the hall and push open the door. Tanya is seated on the toilet with tears in her eyes. Something is wrong. Really wrong."

"Talk to me. What's going on?"

"I'm bleeding a lot. It's like bright red. I think we need to go to the hospital."

She asks for her overnight bag, and I bring it to her. She then tells me to go and warm up my car, while she cleans up.

Within minutes, we are dashing to the emergency room at the hospital a few miles from the house.

"It's going to be all right," I offer, my ignorance of what is going on more than obvious.

"I just don't know if it's my period or something else. My body just feels funny."

I continue talking to her, trying to buoy her mood as best I can.

We arrive at the emergency room, which is partially packed with all manner of accidents, injuries, illnesses, and other craziness that one would expect in the suburbs of Atlanta. After we sign in, we find seats against the back wall.

The room looks sterile, but the sounds of people talking fill the space in a way that makes it feel almost polluted. I help Tanya fill out the paperwork. And then we wait.

When the nurse finally comes out to get Tanya, I ask, "Do you want me to come with you?"

She considers this for a moment, before slowly shaking her head. "I'll be fine. I'll tell them to come back and get you if it turns out to be serious, OK?"

I nod and offer a weak smile.

Watching her walk away, I try to think of all of the possibilities of what is wrong. Not being a doctor, my guessing abilities are fairly limited. All I can do is fixate on her saying that her body felt *funny*.

I take out my phone and google "bright red blood" and "period" and am flooded with a plethora of websites, but one group of websites sticks out: ones detailing miscarriages. I sit up in my chair and take a deep breath. Tanya had mentioned she was on the pill and after that first time we never bothered to protect ourselves. I can barely catch my breath as I allow myself to ponder the possibility that she was pregnant with my child. My face flushes with disbelief and a crushing sadness. Charlotte and I had never attempted children again after Ed Jr. was stillborn. Losing a child fills you with a sadness for which there are no words and we just didn't want to go there again. We had to fight our way back from the bowels of Hell, and every now and then I slip into the darkness a little when I think of my son. When Charlotte became sick, I knew that I would never have a child, and I made my peace with that, choosing instead to focus on my relationship with her. There was no way I could raise a child without her, even if we adopted. In those last years, all of my love was aimed at Charlotte and making her life as comfortable as possible.

As I sit in the waiting room watching patients leave and come in, I notice a large television in the corner of the room. Some syndicated sitcom is running and the volume is turned all the way down with no closed captioning. The minutes pass slowly, as if a miniature man crawled inside of the clock on the wall and held the second hand back with as much force as he could muster before it eventually pushed forward ticking the inevitable change.

Maybe I'm wrong about the miscarriage, but in my gut I don't think that I am. I can't help but to wonder what would have happened if Tanya were still pregnant. What would our lives be like? We are already sneaking around. If we had a child together, there would be no more sneaking, no more hiding. It would also complicate Tanya graduating on time and complicate virtually every aspect of her life. I would probably need to resign from my position at Ellison-Wright and seek out another school to teach at. But even in spite of all those issues, there is a part of me that would have welcomed having a child with Tanya, and I can only believe that it is because I have fallen in love with her.

I stare at the hallway Tanya passed through nearly an hour ago, still waiting, waiting, waiting.

I begin to think that maybe I just got it all wrong. Bleeding could be the result of a heavy period or maybe there was an inflammation of her hemorrhoids. There are probably even more explanations than what I can think of, but my mind keeps falling back on the miscarriage.

I stand and pace around the waiting room before stepping into the hall outside of the emergency room. Restrooms line one side of the hall with a vending area off to the side. A little farther down is a chapel. Directly across the hall is a pharmacy. In the other direction is a bank of elevators and a series of doors that lead to lord knows where.

I walk back into the waiting room and take a seat in the same spot as earlier. Moments later, Tanya walks out, her eyes red and swollen, and I know as she walks up to me and hurls herself into my waiting arms that my worst fears have come true.

## CHAPTER TWENTY-NINE

*No. 45*
*We are the fallen wings of Icarus*
Oh, fuck it.

I OFFER for Tanya to come and stay with me while she recuperates, but she declines, choosing instead to return to her apartment. I have no idea of what her roommate knows about the situation, or even about me in general. In our last conversation she told me that she needed some space and time to think. To that end, she has avoided all contact with me: no phone calls, text messages, instant messages, or even "accidental" encounters at the school. It's as if she is quickly doing away with everything that we have. I want to be there for her, and, frankly, her presence would help mend some of my own sadness over what has happened.

Still it is Tanya who had the complete miscarriage, not I. If she wants space to process things, then I have to respect that, although it has not stopped me from leaving a short message on her cell phone each day to let her know that I love her and that she is not alone.

Weeks later when I finally do hear from her during the middle of December, our relationship is not the focus of the conversation. This time it's about her scholarship.

---

TANYA IS SITTING on the couch on which we made love numerous times, but she is not here for that. There is no overnight bag resting by her feet, only the pensive look of a person trying to solve a riddle that she is ill-equipped to solve alone.

"I was able to make arrangements with most of my professors and make up work that I missed while I was out of class, but Professor Donaldson only let me make up part of my work. He ended up giving me a 'D.' I was hoping that the worst case scenario would have been that he would give me an 'Incomplete.' Now I have a 2.98 and do not qualify for my scholarship."

I don't want to press her about why she didn't attend her classes, especially since I know why. I just wish that she had reached out to me much earlier. I could have probably done much more for her before the grades were issued. At Ellison-Wright College the administration makes it difficult to get grade changes, and when scholarships are lost, they are pretty much lost. But two-hundredths of a point? Surely there was something that could be done.

"The committee will be meeting in a few days before the Christmas break," I say. "I will see what I can do. This is the first time you've ever had any problems with your grades, so they should cut you some slack. Even if you don't have the exact grade point average, your cumulative average is well above the requirement for maintaining your scholarship."

She sighs. "You can do that?"

"I can definitely try really hard."

"Ed, if I don't get my scholarship back, I'm going to have to transfer somewhere else or sit out a semester or more. My mother and I can't afford tuition here without some kind of assistance."

"What about student loans?" I ask.

She shakes her head, lowering it. "Not an option, not since Congress changed the rules for how to get them. Man, I can't believe I really fucked this up."

"Tanya, I promise you I will do everything in my power to help you get back your scholarship." I place my hand on hers, and she allows me to touch her for the first time in nearly five weeks. I have missed the feel of her skin beneath my fingertips. "Can we talk about us?"

She swallows hard and looks away. "I don't hate you for what happened," she starts. "I'm just disappointed in both of us. We took all of this way too far."

"Maybe, but can you think of anything we would have done differently? I can't."

"It doesn't matter." She pauses, and I can see the water building in her eyes. "I was pregnant! Don't you get it? There was a life inside of me that neither one of us planned. What would have happened if I hadn't miscarried? Huh? I would have just been that student that you fucked around with and knocked up. I have plans for my life. I can't believe I was so fucking reckless.

"You know, you asked me was I trying to get even with my dad by having sex with you. I told you no, but I'm starting to wonder what the hell I was thinking to even put myself in the exact same situation my dad was in with Carrie.

"Nothing good could come of this, so we need to just cut our losses. Hey, we had fun. It was cool. But we almost lost our handle on this. Now all I want to do is get my scholarship back and keep my head down and finish my degree. So if you want to do something to help me at this point, help me get my scholarship back, OK? That's all I want from you at this point."

Her words sting, like a blade scraping at my skin, raw and sensitive. "I know that you're hurt. I understand that. I'm hurting, too, but don't think for one second that what we have isn't real. It is *very* real. We are not just two people having a fling. I really care about you. Can you really stand right there and say that you don't love me?"

She starts to open her mouth, but closes it.

"See?" I continue. "When two people love each other, they work through the difficult situations together. That's what I want for us."

"Ed, what's love got to do with it?"

"Everything, Tanya. Everything. Your love saved me."

"From what?"

"From myself," I say, lowering my head. "When my wife passed away, I did not care if something happened to me. I had nothing to live for. You gave me a purpose and showed me that my heart could still hold love. Don't dismiss what we have. You have to give us a chance."

She stands up. "Do you even hear what you're saying? I didn't save your life, and you don't owe me anything. I had a miscarriage, so now we're back to square one. Let's just make a clean split, cut our losses."

"I don't want to do that," I say, rising to my feet.

Tanya kisses me gently on the lips. I can't resist and respond by kissing her deeply. She allows me to, and I sense that we might be backing away from the ledge of our relationship.

"Ed," she says, her lips peeling slowly away from my own, "at this point, it really doesn't matter what you want."

She places her hand against my chest, just above my heart, and then turns around and walks out of my life.

## CHAPTER THIRTY

---

AN HOUR BEFORE THE PRESIDENTIAL SCHOLARSHIP committee meeting is to start I receive a phone call.

"Dr. Nelson?"

"This is he."

"This is Cordell Murphy. You got a minute?"

"Sure," I say, confused as to why he is calling me at all.

"I see that there is one scholarship we won't be renewing today."

"Well, we'll discuss all of that at the meeting."

"It's really a matter of simple mathematics," he says. "If you don't have the grade point average, you don't have the scholarship. Being that you're new to the committee, that might not be so obvious."

God! He's an even bigger ass off the page than he is on it. Still, curiosity keeps me holding my tongue.

"We're meeting in an hour, so to what do I owe this call?" I finally say.

"I'll just cut to the chase. In my capacity as a man of God, I sometimes have to tend to members of my congregation who are sick and shut-in."

"Good for you."

"But not for you, Dr. Nelson."

"What do you mean?"

He pauses for dramatic effect and proceeds to insert the knife slowly and twist it repeatedly. "Well, I was at the hospital a few weeks ago coming out of the chapel when I distinctly saw you ushering a student into the emergency room. The two of you seemed pretty familiar. I didn't realize it was Oreetha Hendrix until I saw the two of you embracing later on. Being that she was crying and you were in a fairly dismal mood yourself, a person doesn't have to be a rocket scientist to know that the two of you had gotten some bad news of an intimate nature."

My heart is beating outside of my chest, but I steady my voice. "You don't know what you're talking about."

"I know that it is very inappropriate for a professor to be romantically involved with a student. Man, that girl isn't even twenty-one yet! What could you have possibly been thinking?"

"It's not what you think," I say, but I can hardly convince myself.

"You are in a position of power and you have used your power to influence a student to engage in illicit behavior with you. Under Title IX that is clearly defined as sexual misconduct. That's far from acceptable for a professor up for tenure next year," he says, his voice bouncing from the joy of his nailing me.

"Why are you doing this?" I ask.

"Oreetha is a good girl, and you, of all people, just lost your wife. I could say it's because of those two things and the flat out disregard for the school policy, which clearly discourages this kind of thing, but if I were to be one hundred percent honest with you, the reason I'm telling you all of this is because I just don't like you."

"You're mad about my paper. I get it. I didn't write it to expressly offend you. I was just recording my research. It wasn't anything personal."

"It was blasphemous, and God is using me to right a wrong here. If you had God in your life, you wouldn't have gotten involved with a student."

Not a single drop of magnanimousness, this fucking prick. "This is not about me," I finally say. "This is about Oreetha and her scholarship and two-hundredths of a point. You know she deserves the benefit of the doubt here."

"Well, Dr. Nelson, 2.98 and 3.0 aren't the same number, are they? If we went around adjusting grade point averages for one person, then we'd have to do it for everyone else, too."

"Do you want me to beg? Is that it?" I ask facetiously.

"That's not necessary. I just want you to resign."

"Are you serious?"

"Do you hear me laughing?" he says.

"And then you'll convince the committee to give Oreetha her scholarship back?"

"That sounds doable."

I remember the look on Tanya's face when she came out of the emergency room, which contrasts so harshly with the look in her eyes when we first made love. I know I will do whatever it takes to make her happy again, and I answer Cordell Murphy reflexively, "I'll resign then."

"Well, make that effective today, and there won't be a need for you at the meeting. You've done enough damage as it is."

When I get off the phone, I am fuming that he destroyed so much of my world in a very short period of time. Although I don't attend church, I know when I meet someone filled with Christian compassion. Cordell Murphy doesn't possess a drop of it anywhere in his pathetic body. The only thing that makes any of this tolerable is that Tanya will get her scholarship back, not that she is even speaking to me.

Maybe it is time that I move on to something else, somewhere else. I never thought a fresh start would be something that I'd ever need. I only wish that I had decided it for myself rather than have someone I despise decide it for me.

## CHAPTER THIRTY-ONE

I TYPE MY LETTER OF RESIGNATION, BUT DECIDE there is no hurry in submitting it. We are going into the Christmas break, which will give me at least two more weeks before I am forced to act. Still, I pack up the few belongings on my desk and head home, careful not to be seen by anyone in the department.

When I get home, I stand in the middle of my den and look around. I have memories of both Charlotte and Tanya in this space now. If these walls could talk, they would tell of love and pain, sadness and joy. This is still my home, and I debate whether or not I could leave it and move somewhere else.

I realize that what I did with Tanya was not acceptable to many people, and I accept my role in that. I'm not someone entirely innocent and can't even pretend to be without some fault in this. But I did what I did for love, and that should make a difference. I loved her and she loved me, and that was real to me. Fuck anyone who can't understand that.

I will never be a saint, but I can be a true friend and a true lover, and to me, that has its own value.

My CELL PHONE rings two days later. This time it's Tanya, and I am guessing she's calling to thank me for helping her get back her scholarship.

"Ed?"

"Yeah?"

"I thought you said you were going to do all that you could to help me get my scholarship back," she says, her voice breaking.

"I did. It's all been taking care of."

"Then why did I get a letter from the committee today saying that my scholarship has been canceled?"

I tell Tanya that I will call her back and then proceed to call the switchboard at Ellison-Wright and have them transfer me to the office of that slimy son of a bitch Cordell Murphy.

"Cordell, what's the deal?" I ask, when he picks up.

"Dr. Nelson, I presume."

"Stop being smug, you asshole. You promised me you would get Oreetha her scholarship back."

"Testy, aren't we? I never said that. I just said that I didn't see why we shouldn't be able to get it back. Apparently, the other committee members thought differently."

"Motherfucker, I should kick your black ass!" I yell, before I realize that threatening him will only compound my problems.

"Don't let the suit and tie fool you," he responds. "I'm from Detroit. The only time I ever got my ass spanked was when the doctor delivered me, and, truth be told, I'm still looking for that dude now."

*Is this really what this situation has devolved to?* I ask myself. *We may as well be slugging it out in the middle of the street.*

"I'm sorry for coming at you like that." I take a deep breath. "I just thought we had an understanding."

"The only understanding we have is that you won't be back next semester," he says.

I smile when I realize that he has no clue I didn't tender my resignation yet. "You're right. You win."

"God wins," he says matter-of-factly.

When I hang up the phone, I call the Ellison-Wright switchboard again. Cordell Murphy might not realize it, but he's incentivized the hell out of me, and I have no intention of going down without a fight.

# CHAPTER THIRTY-TWO

"Hello?"

"Hello, Albert?" I respond. "This is Ed Nelson from African-American Studies."

"Hi, Ed. I'm really sorry to hear about your wife and all. Very sad news."

"Yeah," I offer.

"I don't know if you know this," he says, "but my wife was diagnosed with ovarian cancer a year ago. It was really rough on us, and I can't even begin to wonder what you and your wife must have gone through."

Albert Donaldson and I are not really friends, but I am still relieved at his words. It's not often that you actually end up talking to someone who actually understands what it is like to be the spouse of a person suffering from cancer.

"I appreciate your concern," I finally say. "How is your wife doing?"

"She's in remission now, so we are praying that things remain that way."

"I'll be sure to keep her in my thoughts."

"That's mighty nice of you, Ed," he says. "So what can I do for you?"

I take a deep breath and plow forward. "I'm actually calling on behalf of one your students, actually one of my unofficial advisees, Oreetha Hendrix."

"Oh, yeah. Miss Hendrix. She started out really strong during the first half of the semester, and then things kind of fell apart for her after homecoming. I had heard a lot of great things about her from other faculty in the department, so I was surprised when she came up short in my class. Guess all that sorority stuff can be a bit distracting," Albert says.

"That's actually what I wanted to talk with you about. She has been confiding in me throughout the semester, and while I'm not at liberty to say what she has been going through, I can vouch for the fact that she had an emergency to come up that she was ill-equipped to handle emotionally."

"Frankly, I'm surprised that she didn't get an official excuse from the Dean of Women. Our policy is to deal directly with that office and let them vet the students' excuses. That way we don't get into a situation where students start lying to get over on the professors," he says.

"I understand completely. I've had similar issues with students myself. But this situation is a bit different, a bit more delicate. I'm sure she would have gone to the Dean of Women if she had been thinking more clearly. Hey, I'm not trying to make excuses for her, but I wanted you to have a greater understanding of what her situation has been."

Albert sighs heavily. "So you want me to change her grade to an 'Incomplete.' Is that it?"

"I just want you give her the benefit of the doubt. She's a good student, one of the best I've ever dealt with here at Ellison-Wright. She's here on one of the presidential scholarships, and the grade she received from your class brought her GPA down by two-hundredths of a point from keeping her scholarship."

"Two-hundredths of a point? Are you trying to tell

me the scholarship committee couldn't work with her over that sliver of points?" he says, mildly incredulous.

I take this as a good sign.

"I'm on the committee," I respond. "I am in favor of it, but other members of the committee are far more skeptical."

"Just curious, but who else is on the committee?"

"Cordell Murphy," I start.

"Oh please!"

Now I am completely intrigued.

"He *is* quite the character," I say, nudging Albert to say more.

"I'm sorry. I don't mean to talk ill of other professors, but I'm guessing you know that he's a jackass or else we probably wouldn't be having this conversation."

I laugh. "You could say that."

"He's always so much holier than thou," Albert continues. "Talking down to people and that fool is married to his own cousin, or at least that's what I hear."

My jaw drops. This is something I wouldn't normally entertain, but now I am in a street fight with a guy who wants to not only destroy me, but take down Tanya, too. No information is too sacred to not be used as ammunition at this point.

"His cousin? What like a third cousin or something?"

"More like a first cousin."

"Naw, I can't believe that. Is that even legal?" I ask.

"Hell, I don't know. I'm not a lawyer, but I don't think Georgia has a law against cousins getting together. After all, this *is* the deep South."

I laugh, still floored by the comment and the casual way in which he has tossed it out there.

"Well," I continue, "he's the hold up, which is why I'm calling you now. I know this is a big favor to ask of you, and I know you have a ton of things already on your plate, but is there any way she could make up some of her work next semester and get an 'Incomplete'? I would consider this a personal favor. She's a good student who is just getting over a very difficult time in her life."

"I see," he responds. "If you don't mind me asking, what happened to her?"

His question should not surprise me, given the way he gossips about other professors, but it does. I feel like he's on the verge of giving me what I called for, so I know I will have to tell him something.

"Things of a feminine nature," I say, cautiously. "But it's benign," I add.

The word "benign" is a loaded word, I know, but I need to both silence his curiosity and still appeal to his sense of understanding. I am not above playing on his emotions at this point. Although this conversation is going well, I cannot lie to myself and say he is actually a friend of mine, no matter how he is acting at the moment.

"I see," he responds, his voice somber. He pauses for several seconds before continuing, "I'll process the paperwork for the grade change. Let her know that she will have to make everything up at the beginning of the spring semester."

"Sure. No problem. And thank you," I say.

"Hey, no problem, Ed," he responds. "I might need to call on a favor from *you* one day."

I hesitate to think what that might be, but I agree.

"Take care, and give my best to your wife," I offer.

"You take care, too."

# CHAPTER THIRTY-THREE

ALTHOUGH IT PAINS ME TO CALL CORDELL Murphy back, I do. I tell him that Albert Donaldson is issuing an "Incomplete" for Tanya and that I am officially notifying the committee that her GPA is now in good standing. None of this pleases Cordell, but, frankly, I couldn't give a flying fuck. I then tell him that there is a rumor going around about his wife being his first cousin. I realize this is incredibly petty on my part, and I am only using this bit of information out of spite. Still, when I say this to him, the conversation tenses up incredibly.

"Where did you hear that?" he asks.

It is at this point that I know it is true.

"It doesn't matter. I'm not one to spread gossip about other people's personal lives. And I'm guessing you aren't the kind of person to spread gossip about other people's personal lives, either."

He is quiet for what feels like an eternity.

"Well, I guess neither one of us has any interest in gossiping about mere speculations, right?"

"Right."

Again, we are silent.

I want to say something that will bury the hatchet between the two of us, but my gut is saying that our truce on the matter in no way connotes a desire for us to be friends. He will continue being him, and I will continue being me. The only difference is that he'll have to keep his punches above the belt going forward.

Outside of that, I couldn't care less about what is going on in his world.

---

THE SUN IS BEGINNING to set and an auburn hue punctuates the horizon. Few things are more beautiful than dusk in spring, the cicadas roaring buzz in the distance with crickets chirping in syncopation. Tanya arrives minutes before seven, dressed in denim shorts and a baby t-shirt with her sorority letters across the front.

"Need any help with that?" I ask, through my open front door.

"I got it," she responds. "It's just one bag."

She brings the bag to the door and I insist that she lets me set up its contents.

"Well, if you insist," she says with a smile.

The bag contains whole fried catfish, French fries, hushpuppies, and a sweet potato pie. I smile when I see the food, remembering the first time Tanya cooked for me. This meal is her way of thanking me for helping her get back her scholarship.

"OK," she says, once our plates are set. "Now you have to tell me how you did it."

"Don't worry about it. I just made a few phone calls. It wasn't that difficult."

"That wasn't our agreement," she says, smiling. "You promised you would tell me everything once we made it to spring break. I thought that you said you would always be straight up with me. Are you going against your word?"

"Oh so you're going to make this about my word?"

I say, chuckling. "My word is that I love you, so there was nothing I wouldn't have done to fix that situation."

She stares at me for a moment. "So you still love me?"

"I never stopped."

She allows this information to wash over her before continuing, "You're changing the subject, Ed. Now tell me what happened or else I'm going to pack up all of this delicious fish and take it back and give to my greedy ass roommate."

"OK," I say, stifling my laughter.

I tell her as much of the story that is reasonable to share. She doesn't need to have every last detail. Just the basics.

She nods and I am unable to read her thoughts. She returns to her meal and we continue eating dinner in silence. Once we finish, Tanya nudges me playfully, gradually coming to life.

"What?" I ask.

"So what do we do now?"

"What do you mean?"

She shrugs. "With us."

"That depends on if you still love me."

She takes a moment to consider this before responding, "I believe that I do."

"You want to try again?"

"Maybe we should just take this thing really slow, OK? Let's try just being friends for a while and leave the other stuff out. Could you deal with that?"

"I can deal with any situation that allows me to be a part of your life."

We put our dishes in the sink and walk over to the den, taking a seat on the couch. I turn on the television, and Tanya lays her head on my shoulder.

"What's on?" she asks.

"Don't know, but it doesn't really matter."

"I guess not."

The TV watches us.

---

*No. 60*

*Can the heart ever heal from loss*
*And yield to the newness of love*
*Born of the need to feel alive?*
*I hold on to hope like helium*
*Locked against the walls of a balloon*
*Trying not to drift away, far from*
*This place that we once called home.*

- fin -

## ALSO BY RAN WALKER

# ABOUT THE AUTHOR

Ran Walker is the author of sixteen books. His work has appeared in a variety of anthologies and journals.

Ran's novel *Daykeeper* is the winner of the 2018 Virginia Indie Author Project Award, the 2019 National Indie Author of the Year Award, and the Black Caucus of the American Library Association Best Fiction Ebook Award.

He and his family live in Virginia, where he works as a creative writing professor at Hampton University. He can be reached via his website, www.ranwalker.com.